"Take cover!"

Nick hollered and dove on top of Ruby.

Another bullet slammed into the earth. Nick held her tight as they rolled together down the hill away from the bullets.

Somewhere in the trees, the shooter had found them. Again.

Nick wasn't sure if the better option was to run toward the cabin or try to get around the pond while they had the hill to safeguard them.

"Let's stay along the edge of the hill and move toward the cabin," Ruby said.

"We're not safe anywhere."

* * *

Pacific Northwest K-9 Unit

Books by Jessica R. Patch

Love Inspired Suspense

Pacific Northwest K-9 Unit

Cold Case Revenge

Quantico Profilers

Texas Cold Case Threat
Cold Case Killer Profile
Texas Smoke Screen

Cold Case Investigators

Cold Case Takedown
Cold Case Double Cross
Yuletide Cold Case Cover-Up

Love Inspired Trade

Her Darkest Secret
A Cry in the Dark

Visit the Author Profile page at LoveInspired.com for more titles.

COLD CASE REVENGE

JESSICA R. PATCH

LOVE INSPIRED SUSPENSE
INSPIRATIONAL ROMANCE

Special thanks and acknowledgment are given to Jessica R. Patch
for her contribution to the Pacific Northwest K-9 Unit miniseries.

LOVE INSPIRED® SUSPENSE
INSPIRATIONAL ROMANCE

ISBN-13: 978-1-335-59756-4

Cold Case Revenge

Recycling programs
for this product may
not exist in your area.

Love Inspired
22 Adelaide St. West, 41st Floor
Toronto, Ontario M5H 4E3, Canada
www.LoveInspired.com

Printed in U.S.A.

For there is hope of a tree, if it be cut down,
that it will sprout again, and that the tender branch
thereof will not cease.
—*Job* 14:7

To a wonderful friend and author, Jodie Bailey.
I feel like this book is apropos for reasons you and I
only know (giggle)! Here's to many more years of writing,
laughing, praying, retreats in the Outer Banks
and sharing daughter stories. You're a Rockstar.

Special thanks to Emily Rodmell for editing this book and
allowing me to be a part of this wonderful K-9 continuity.
It's been so much fun. And to the contributing authors
whom I've collaborated with. I've enjoyed getting to know
all of you so much better!

ONE

Nick Rossi glanced up at the pewter sky and snatched his Stetson before it blew off his head into the gust of wind that rolled off Lake Chelan. Lake Chelan National Recreation Area rested in a glacially carved trough in the Cascade Range of Washington state and took one's breath away. It was only *one* of the reasons that Nick had settled in Stehekin Valley.

"It gonna rain, Daddy?" his three-year-old daughter, Zoe, asked as her service dog, Goldie, licked the caramel from her half-eaten apple on a stick. She'd gone almost five months without a seizure, and Nick thanked God for it. Zoe had been diagnosed with epilepsy at nine months old then they'd lost her mom, Penelope, three months later in a car accident. Rubbing the bare spot on his left ring finger, he shook off the painful memories and surveyed the recreational area.

The open grounds, flanked by evergreens, was set up with food trucks, crafts, games, vendor tents and a live bluegrass band. He hadn't always loved bluegrass, but then his friend Jodie had introduced him to the band Steep Canyon Rangers. Not even the music could soothe him at the moment, and most everyone wore the same expression as Nick.

Grim.

Rain might be an understatement if the rolling thunderclouds had anything to say about it. Local news had forecasted possible storms later today, but it appeared the weather had a mind of its own and didn't care to listen to meteorologists and hold off.

"It gonna rain, Daddy?" Zoe asked again, this time tugging on his hand, which was sticky from her earlier cotton candy and caramel. She was going to be sick from all the sugar.

"I think so, baby girl. We better play a whole lot before it does."

"Yay! Me and Goldie want to paint. Can we?" She pointed to an open tent with a green canvas roof. Preschool-sized easels and finger paints filled the area the Arts & Humanities of Stehekin had concocted for young artists.

"Of course, you can. Let's go." He led her to the tent and an easel, then helped her into a painting smock and ordered Goldie to place. The sweet retriever dropped at Zoe's feet at the command, watching patiently. With Zoe being too young to qualify for a service dog, Nick had trained her himself…with some help from a friend who had knowledge about teaching service dogs. Goldie was now skilled to sense when Zoe might lapse into a seizure and alert Nick in time for him to help his daughter from falling and hurting herself. Sometimes she fell fast, though, and if that happened, Goldie would position herself to buoy Zoe's fall. Then she'd remain by Zoe's side and lick her little leg. Nick was convinced Goldie loved Zoe completely and wholly. Exactly how Nick loved his baby girl.

Zoe dipped her fingers in the green paint. "I'm gonna make the trees."

"That will be very pretty."

"And our horsies."

"Perfect."

Thunder rumbled again and the clouds grew soggier. The lake wind was chilly and damp, and the firs, spruces and pines rustled. The painting paper whipped upward on easels and kids squealed, including Zoe.

The Lady of the Lake ferry cruised down the fifty miles of Lake Chelan toward the Cascade Mountains. The peaks glistened with early snow that hadn't reached the valley yet. Overhead speakers warned tourists that the weather was getting rough on the river and the ferry would only travel once more—weather permitting.

The only way into Stehekin was by plane, boat or on horseback. This storm could easily strand tourists and there wouldn't be enough lodging for everyone. Not to mention they'd have no real way of communicating unless they owned a satellite phone, which most tourists did not. Very few in Stehekin had them. Business owners, mostly.

The horse outfitter he owned, Cascades Stables, had horses out on trails with guides. They provided day rides to loop rides, camping adventures and family picnics. He used his sat phone to check in with his employees and to make sure they were cutting the trip short. Which would mean refunds or rain checks.

He stepped out from under the tent, a few feet away from Zoe, and watched her paint. Goldie was alert but lying quietly at her feet. Candy, his former main trail guide now manager, answered.

"Hey, boss."

"Checking in. Storm is coming fast. Ferries are taking a last call."

"Yeah, we felt some rain so we headed in, and I rain-checked them."

"Good deal. Take care of the others for me, would you?"

"Say that again. Storm's messing with your reception."

He turned and glanced at Zoe, who was now dipping a paintbrush into a little plastic cup. He repeated himself then ended the call. Candy had been with him for about four years. A year younger than his own thirty-three, Candy had become the manager and his right hand around the stables since Penelope's death. He'd fallen off the deep end and she'd picked up the business slack and helped with Zoe. She hadn't minded, said it kept her busy and gave her and her husband, Garrett, good parenting practice for when they had their own family.

"Excuse me," a woman said and pointed at his gray T-shirt with his business logo printed in the center. "Do you work for Cascades Stables?"

"I own it, yes."

She grinned, then pointed in the distance to a little boy standing with a man Nick assumed to be the child's dad. "My son wants to ride horses before we leave, and I heard you start at age three. Do you think we could set something up?"

"I'm sure we can." He patted his pockets and realized he'd left his business cards at home. "I was going to give you the number, but I don't have a card." Instead, he quickly gave her directions, operation hours and prices. No Wi-Fi in Stehekin except for at the Stehekin Lodge, which only had limited access.

"Let me write that down or I'll forget. I have a note-book in my purse." She released the strap from her shoulder and unzipped her bag, and he glanced over at Zoe painting. The purse clattered to the ground, diverting his attention as the contents spilled out. "I am so clumsy. I'll probably fall off a horse within five minutes." She kneeled down and Nick followed suit. He handed her a pen and a set of keys.

"We give a small learning course for beginners. You'll be fine," he said.

She took her items and shoved them inside her purse, then grabbed her little notebook. "That number."

"Just a second." He turned back. His heart hiccupped and his breath left his lungs.

Zoe and Goldie were gone.

Missing child. The words continued to hit Pacific Northwest K-9 Officer Ruby Orton's gut like a cement block against a crystal vase.

A preschooler in North Cascades National Park. Three years old. Epileptic. The little girl had had her service dog, a golden retriever, with her when she disappeared, but the dog hadn't responded to calls from the father or the park rangers. That unsettled Ruby as she shifted in her seat in the floatplane that was carrying them to Stehekin Valley.

The child might have been abducted, and something harmful could have happened to the service dog. Something Ruby refused to imagine. She glanced down at her working dog, Pepper. The black Lab had been with her for four years, and they were inseparable. Pepper was her best friend and an excellent trail-tracking, search-and-rescue dog.

"This weather isn't going to make things easy," Tanner Ford, her PNK9 colleague, said as he scratched the ears of his boxer, Britta. She, too, was adept at tracking missing persons. According to the park ranger who radioed them, the father was borderline hysterical.

Ruby understood. North Cascades was over five hundred thousand acres, and risks of falling, drowning or even being attacked by wild animals abounded. The rugged, steep, glacial terrain was hard enough on experienced hikers and visitors to the park. A child alone… Ruby shuddered.

"Hey, don't think like that yet," Tanner said, as if knowing exactly where her thoughts were going.

"Hard not to. It's a little girl who was painting and playing, then gone."

"I know. I know," he said quietly and rubbed Britta's ears.

Pepper nestled closer to Ruby as the floatplane jostled them through the rough air currents. "Hold fast, back there," Dylan Jeong, their other PNK9 colleague, called as he piloted them toward Lake Chelan, to eventually land in Stehekin Valley. His Saint Bernard, Ridge, sat as his copilot in a leather harness that had the words *Bad for the Bones* on it. Dylan's dog was as cool and admired as Dylan himself. Ridge was skilled in mountain rescue, and they needed all hands and paws on deck.

Ruby wasn't a fan of boats, and they didn't have four hours, which was the length of time it would have taken had they chosen water over air. She'd fallen off a boat when she was twelve and the trauma never left her. But she did her job and if it meant traveling by ferry, she'd do it like the strong South Alabama woman her mama and grandmama had raised her to be. She might live outside North Cascades now, but it would take more than four years living here to take the Mobile out of this girl.

As the small plane made its descent to the choppy waters, Ruby held tight to Pepper. "Ready to work, girl?"

Pepper licked her hand in response. Pepper lived for the work and was her best friend. Too bad she couldn't go back in time, or Ruby would have paid attention to Pepper's cues concerning her ex-boyfriend, Eli Ballard. His business partner, Stacey Stark, and her boyfriend, Jonas Digby, had been gunned down this past April in Mount Rainier National Park, and PNK9's rookie crime-scene investigator, Mara Gilmore, had been the prime suspect from the get-go. The ex-girlfriend of the male victim, she'd been seen looming over the body, then fleeing from the murder site and been on the run ever since.

But the team had recently discovered that Eli might be involved. He'd been so charming and sweet. Ruby had instantly liked him when they'd met during the early investigation. Pepper hadn't warmed up to him, though, and maybe that should have been a clue. Though she chalked it up to Pepper being a little jealous. And that still might be the case. Either way, Ruby had had no choice but to end things with Eli.

She'd done it subtly, but lamely, through a text, in case he was connected to the murders, so as not to tip him off that they were looking at him as a person of interest. Truth was, her work schedule *was* getting in the way, which is what she'd used as her excuse. Besides their normal day-to-day routines, the PNK9 unit was working 24/7 to find Mara and to work the Stark/Digby case as well as searching for the three bloodhound pups they'd been training for scent work.

The cases hadn't given Ruby much time for a romantic relationship, but she'd attempted one with Eli, thinking she might be able to fall in love with him. Now, she was pretty disappointed in herself because Eli might be a slick liar. Per the investigation, the team was operating on the assumption that Mara Gilmore was in hiding because the *real* killer had threatened her father, who was in a memory-care unit in a nursing home. A man fitting Eli's description had visited that same home, and Eli Ballard had no other reason to be there.

Ruby sighed. She'd yet to pick a romantic winner.

People often did irrational things when it came to love—even murder. And sadly, Mara fit the bill for killing Stacey Stark and Jonas Digby, though it was a hard pill to swallow. Mara did have a strong motive—she and Jonas had dated before he began seeing Stacey, and Mara had been heartbroken by the breakup. A week later Stacey and Jonas had been found shot to death and Mara looming over their bodies. Since April she'd been MIA. Still…innocent until proven guilty, and the team had been tracking leads—now, especially Eli Ballard—while searching for Mara.

Ruby shook away the thoughts and focused on the missing little girl. As if reading her mind again, Tanner sighed. "We'll find her, and we'll get to the truth."

"I know." He was right. She pointed to his head, where he'd been shot just barely a month ago. Thankfully it had been a minor wound only requiring stitches, but that proved just how serious all their cases were. "I just hope it doesn't kill us."

"I hear ya." He laughed but this was no joking matter.

The plane's landing upon Lake Chelan wasn't pleasant, but they made it to the dock and she exited with Pepper, Tanner and Britta behind her, then Dylan and Ridge joined them. They donned their green PNK9 windbreakers, and Ruby slipped on the hood as it began to drizzle.

She clutched Pepper's leash and straightened her harness, which had PNK9 in black lettering on each side.

They were met by two North Cascades National Park rangers, who quickly gave them the details of the missing child as they all jumped inside two Polaris Rangers. The wind rocked the vehicles as they drove toward Lake Chelan National Recreation Area, where the Labor Day festival was being held and where the child had vanished. They maneuvered the terrain and Ruby spotted several bright-colored tents as they approached. It looked like many had already evacuated due to the storm.

A muscular man with a cowboy hat clutched in one hand paced as he raked his dark, almost black, hair with his free hand. No doubt that was the dad who had lost the child. While fear lined his face, she also noticed frustration—probably with himself. Parents typically blamed themselves. But even as he paced, his gait was smooth, as if this manner was the way he processed tough situations.

Ruby jumped from the vehicle and calmly strode ahead with purpose, Tanner and Dylan flanking her. "Mr. Rossi?" she asked and extended her hand first since she was the lead on this. "I'm Officer Ruby Orton with the Pacific Northwest K-9 unit. This is Officer Ford and Officer Jeong. And these are Pepper, Britta and Ridge. We'll be searching for your daughter, and we don't want to waste time."

He shook her hand with a firm grip and his ice-blue eyes met hers. His square jaw twitched. "Thank you. She has epilepsy, and stress and anxiety can trigger a seizure. We have very little time to find her." He spoke with authority, but she heard the fear in his tone.

"We will do our very best and move quickly, but I have to ask a few questions, Mr. Rossi."

"I know. Let's just get them done so we can cover the

terrain. The last time I saw Zoe was almost an hour ago over there by that easel. I had stepped out from under the tent because I needed a satellite signal to check on my employees. They were giving horseback tours today. Weather is… Zoe hates storms." His eyes filled with moisture. "She'll be afraid if the thunder gets louder."

As if on cue, it did.

Her heart felt for him. He was doing an excellent job of keeping it together. And he was right. The weather was not on their side—it was working against them.

He continued without her redirection. "I called my employee, Candy Reynolds. Then a woman approached me about horseback riding for her son. She dropped her purse, and I kneeled to help her pick up the items. It wasn't but a few seconds. Then I turned and Zoe was gone, and Goldie, too." The girl's service dog. A golden retriever. "She hasn't responded to my calls or dog whistles. That's unlike her."

That's what had Ruby rattled. She glanced at Tanner, then at Dylan, and they both wore grim expressions.

"Well, our dogs are highly trained, and we should get them started now. I need an item that belongs to Zoe. Something that she alone would have and not carry any transference from anyone else."

He nodded. "I have her 'lovey.' It's a baby blanket she carries and sleeps with. It may have my scent on it from putting it in the backpack, but only she uses it."

Ruby took the worn pink-and-purple blanket and put it in front of Pepper. "Scent, Pepper." The dog sniffed at the blanket then looked at Nick Rossi. She'd caught his scent. "Scent, Pepper," she said again, letting the dog know that she wanted the other scent tracked.

Pepper sniffed again and sat, which let Ruby know

she had it and was ready. Ruby then passed the blanket to Tanner and Dylan, and they gave their dogs the scent. Once all the K-9s were ready to work, Ruby patted Pepper. She would move fast, so she made sure she had the twenty-foot leash on her, just as Dylan and Tanner had on their dogs.

"You can come with us, Mr. Rossi, if you like, but please don't get in Pepper's or the other dogs' way."

"I won't. Thank you."

"Ready?"

Tanner and Dylan nodded.

"Track, Pepper," she called sternly, and Pepper's nose hit the ground as she sniffed her way to the tent where Zoe had been painting. She paused, then sniffed again and moved to the other side of the tent, out the back area and through the crowd heading east. The two park rangers drove alongside them in their UTV.

A gust of wind kicked up and Pepper paused, raised her head in the air and sniffed. "Did she lose the scent?" Nick asked. He was jogging along with them, unable to sit in the UTV. Ruby understood nervous energy.

"No, she's just catching the right one." She didn't explain that patience was required. His daughter was in this harsh area alone, or with a dog…or with someone. *Patience* wouldn't be a word he'd want to hear and she wouldn't be trite. "Track, Pepper."

Pepper began again, briskly, across the rocks and terrain that dipped between the jagged peaks of the mountains. Ruby worked to keep up on the loose rock.

Suddenly the leash was no longer taut. Pepper must have sat—her alert.

"What is she doing? What's she found?" Nick asked, his voice wobbly. Ruby put out her arm.

"Please stay still, Mr. Rossi." Ruby glanced at Tanner and he called Britta to him, then sidled up next to Nick to keep him from following Ruby. Just in case the worst-case scenario was up ahead.

Dylan followed her. Both dogs had alerted and were sitting up on the crest of the trail—sitting beside a small pink tennis shoe. If Pepper and Ridge were alerting, the shoe belonged to Zoe Rossi, or she'd had it in her possession.

"That what I think it is?" Dylan asked and rubbed Ridge's head. "Good boy, Ridge."

"Yeah. We're less than half a mile from the event. Rugged terrain. If she wandered away, how did she end up here? Why not just mosey around all the other booths and games?"

Dylan sighed. "Because she might not have wandered."

Ruby snapped a photo with her cell-phone camera, since the park's crime-scene investigator wasn't here... yet. They could download it later when they had Wi-Fi access. She surveyed the area. Below the crest was a huge lake. She rubbed Pepper's head.

"Officer!" Nick called. "Did you...? Is she...?" His voice broke.

"I hate this part of the job," Ruby whispered.

"Same."

"No, but you can come up." Might as well let him identify the shoe as Zoe's, or not.

Nick, the rangers in the UTV, Tanner and Britta hurried up and Nick paused when he saw the shoe.

"Oh, no. No." He fell to his knees and picked up the shoe, clutching it to his chest.

Ruby clenched her teeth to hold back the emotion about to erupt from her eyes. "Mr. Rossi," she murmured.

"Don't go there yet, okay? Just…hold on a little longer for us."

She patted Pepper. "Good girl. Track, Pepper."

Pepper left the shoe and continued her search as Ruby prayed they'd find the little girl alive and well. The missing shoe didn't give her much hope, but she refused to let the father see that. He needed hope. Pepper continued her trek up the crest and through a dense area of trees that opened up to a small clearing that overlooked Lake Chelan.

A black-tailed doe ran across the trail, but the dogs ignored it. Pepper sniffed to the edge of the cliff and sat, alerting her. Ruby saw nothing. But something was here. Ridge and Britta also alerted.

"What am I missing?" Ruby asked.

Tanner and Dylan, who were searching the foliage and behind trees, both shook their heads.

"Below is a ledge," Nick said and hurried to the edge. He stretched out on the ground and hung his head over. "Oh, baby! Zoe!" he hollered.

"Hey, Daddy!" a tiny, scared voice called. "I was waiting on you."

Relief flooded Ruby, but the situation wasn't over yet. She joined Nick on the forest floor. Five feet below was a narrow grassy strip where the little girl was sitting with her golden retriever nestled beside her. How in the world did she get down there?

"I wost my shoe."

If she moved any closer to the edge, she could fall into the lake or on jagged rocks below. Ruby's heart rate sped up. Before she could devise a plan, Nick was already lowering himself down.

* * *

Nick's hands were shaking, and his heart banged against his ribs as he stared down at his baby girl sitting still, but so close to the edge, even with Goldie acting as a barrier between the cliff's edge and Zoe. He loved that dog.

"Be real still, baby. Okay?" Nick lowered himself down. The ledge was sturdy and secure, but he wasted no time. He grabbed his daughter; her hair had matted to her cheeks from rain and possibly tears. But she was now safe, and he thanked the Good Lord.

When she'd disappeared, he'd been in a panic, but had then forced himself to go into investigator mode from his military-police days, when he worked for the Criminal Investigations Division. But this wasn't one of the children victims' cases he'd been assigned to at the military base. This was his daughter. Those crimes he'd seen so often always reminded him of the worst day of his life.

This couldn't have happened again.

He'd been so careful with Zoe. Overprotective. He'd even bought a backpack with a leash on it to make sure she didn't get away when she'd learned to walk. It was like his little sister, Lizzie, all over again. But his daughter had been found.

His sister never had.

He lifted up Zoe, and the agent—Ruby—took her. "It's okay, baby girl. She is going to help you."

Ruby smiled, her big brown eyes radiating compassion and relief. Her smile was wide, revealing a set of dimples in her light brown cheeks. A few raindrops ran down the side of her face, but she didn't seem to mind.

"I got ya, darlin', so don't worry. You're okay," the pretty officer said and he noticed her Southern accent. Once Zoe was secure, the agent grabbed her satellite phone and a few seconds later let her team know that Zoe had been found safe. He could hear cheering on the other end of the line.

He lifted up Goldie and the two male officers helped him. Then he hoisted himself up and took back Zoe, hugging her to him. "How did you get out here? Did you get lost?"

"I did just as her said. I was hided good."

His blood turned to ice. "Who said?"

"The wady who's your friend. She said we was pwaying hide-and-seek. She helped me hide and said you'd find me. You did find me, Daddy! You winned." She squished his cheeks with her hands and kissed him right on the nose. "But I don't know what you winned."

"Do you know the nice lady who brought you out here, Zoe?" Ruby asked.

"No. I felled and wost my shoe."

"We need to get to shelter. It's about to blow up," Ruby said. The sky had turned a deep inky shade and thunder boomed. Behind the ominous clouds, lightning shot through the horizon.

"I'd like to see if Britta can track the abductor. I don't want to lose the scent due to rain. If I move fast—"

"I'll help. Cover more ground," Dylan said, and Tanner nodded.

"We might be able to pick up the scent. Find her."

Ruby nodded. "Be careful."

Tanner squatted. "Zoe, this is Britta. And Britta would like to sniff you. It might even tickle. Can she do that?"

Zoe nodded.

Britta and the other dog both sniffed his daughter, then their handlers gave them the cue and the dogs immediately went to work, ignoring the thunder and lightning.

One UTV went with the two officers, and one stayed behind with them.

"Let's go," the ranger said.

"If we don't hurry, a downpour could get us into a mudslide," Nick hollered over the whistling wind. Ruby pulled a poncho from her gear bag and covered Zoe. Zoe shivered against him, and he held her tight.

"It's okay. You're safe."

But a woman had guided her away and hid her on a cleft where she could have fallen and died. Who would have done this?

And why?

His parents calling for Lizzie flashed in his mind. Their frantic eyes and voices. The terror of that day gripped him. He now knew what his parents had experienced. Those memories came raging back, though they'd never truly left him…

"Where's Lizzie?" Mom had asked.

"She had to potty. She's in the bathroom with you," Nick said.

Dad walked up. "What's going on?" He handed Nick an ice-cream cone and held the one for Lizzie in his other hand. "Where's your sister?"

Mom rushed into the bathroom.

Nick's heart beat too hard. Too fast. It hurt inside his chest.

Mom bolted from the bathroom, her face as white as snow. "She's gone! She's gone, David!"

Ice cream ran down Nick's arm. He couldn't eat it. Couldn't even look at it.

And he'd never eaten ice cream again…

Not once in the almost twenty-five years since Lizzie had disappeared from the North Cascades National Park.

TWO

Ruby shivered as she stood inside Nick Rossi's large A-frame cabin-like home that was located in the Stehekin community near his Cascades Stables. Not long after they'd arrived, the storm hit with extreme ferocity, and she hoped Tanner and Dylan had made it to the ranger station or somewhere safe. They hadn't called her yet. With the terrible weather, it was affecting the phones' signals.

The home was tastefully decorated in earth tones with a few feminine touches. Probably from a wife, who didn't seem to be in the picture. He didn't wear a ring, but had rubbed the spot absently, which clued her in that his singleness was recent.

"Could I find a place to change?" She kept a bag with her for instances like this. One never knew what would happen in a national park. The weather and circumstances were often unpredictable.

Nick shook his head. "I'm sorry. I'm out of sorts. Sure." He pointed upstairs. "I have a guest room. First door on the right with a bathroom. You'll find all you need." A crack of thunder rattled the windows, and Ruby sighed.

As she entered the room, which had a queen-size bed, Nick hollered that she had a phone call from Officer Ford.

She picked up the receiver of the old-school phone on the night table and answered, then heard Nick hang up the downstairs receiver.

"Hey, Tanner. I was about to call you," she said. "When the stormed passed that is."

"It's nasty out. We had a trail, but we lost it. Had no choice but to turn back. We're at the park ranger's station. Dylan says we can't fly in this weather so we're gonna bunk in a room here. You safe?"

Ruby wished they'd had better weather. They might have found the person behind the abduction. "Yeah. The park ranger brought us back to Mr. Rossi's house. I want to ask him a few more questions while everything is still fresh, and he wanted to get Zoe home, where she feels most comfortable, due to her seizures. If the storm lets up soon, I'll see if I can get a room at the Stehekin Lodge."

"It's not going to anytime soon. Not to overstep, since you're the lead on the case, but I called the chief and filled him in."

Ruby shrugged out of her jacket and Pepper rested by the sliding glass door that led to a private balcony. "No, I'm glad. Anything new on Mara?"

"No," Tanner said softly. "Still no word." Ruby knew that Tanner was good friends with Mara's brother, Asher Gilmore, a fellow officer at the PNK9. The case had been hard on all of them, but particularly Asher. Mara and Asher were half siblings but hadn't grown up together and had recently started to develop a bond as colleagues *and* family when she'd gone into hiding.

"What about the puppies?" Ruby asked. Three months ago, the three bloodhound puppies that PNK9 head trainer Peyton Burns had been preparing for specialization in scent detection had been stolen from the play yard and the team had been trying to track the culprits. They thought they had a solid lead on a backyard breeder as the thief, but it turned out to be false. The whole team was worried. The bloodhound pups were almost ready to become fully trained K-9s.

"Nothing so far. I asked. Keep me posted on where you'll be for the night."

"Will do." She hung up and changed into dry clothing, then padded down the wooden staircase, which had real log beams for railings, toward the scent of fresh coffee. Pepper followed. The kitchen was full of stainless steel, granite counters and rustic cabinetry, giving the place a cozy feel.

"You like coffee?"

"That's like asking if I like breathing."

Nick grinned and poured two cups of coffee while Zoe drew at the kitchen table. Goldie was lying by her chair, watching her. Zoe's bare foot petted Goldie's back. The row of floor-to-ceiling windows, which on a normal day would undoubtedly reveal a breathtaking view, showed nothing but an ominous landscape. Torrential rain beat on the glass panes and trees bent dangerously to the ground.

"How do you take your coffee, Officer Orton?"

"Ruby. Please. And cream is fine if you have it." She ambled to the kitchen table and studied the picture Zoe was earnestly working on, the tip of her little tongue touching her upper lip as she concentrated. It appeared to be a big mountain—done in purple—with a big blue lake below. A stick figure with yellow hair and a pink shirt, or maybe a jacket, held a little girl's hand and Goldie stood next to the girl, who must have been Zoe.

"You are a very good drawer, Zoe," Ruby said and pointed to the dog. "Is that Goldie?"

"Yep."

She pointed to the little girl with pink shoes. "Is that you?"

"Yep," she said with an exaggerated nod.

"And who is this?" She pointed to the woman with yellow hair and the pink shirt or jacket.

"That's my friend."

"What is your friend's name?" Ruby asked.

"Just friend. She said she was my friend and Daddy's friend and she wanted to pway hide-and-seek with me."

Zoe clearly didn't know the woman or she would have used a name. Didn't mean the woman didn't know Nick. She could have used a clever disguise. Zoe was three. She'd have easily been duped. "Was she tall, like me?" Ruby was almost six feet without her shoes. She'd taken after her dad's side of the family, though she'd never known them. He and Mama had never married. And by the time Ruby was five, he was completely out of the picture.

"No, her wasn't tall wike you."

Nick handed her a cup of coffee and grinned. "It's strong."

"Perfect." She noticed his popping blue eyes again and that he was a few inches taller than her, putting him at six-three, at least.

"Why don't we sit in the living room where we can have a little space. I don't want Zoe to hear anything…" Then he mouthed *scary*.

Everything about this was scary. "I agree." The living area was open to the kitchen and Nick chose an oversize chair facing the table, so he could see Zoe's every move. Ruby took the love seat and Pepper followed, sitting at her feet.

"Any news from your colleagues?" Nick asked.

"They lost the trail. Had to stop due to the storm. They'll be staying at the ranger's station overnight."

"But they had a scent?"

"They did."

She sat quietly, sipping her coffee and letting him process the fact that they'd lost the person who took his daughter. Finally, she spoke. "Zoe doesn't know who took her. That doesn't mean you don't know. Do you have any enemies? Anyone who might want to do you or Zoe harm? Business competitors?"

Nick raked a hand through his thick, ebony hair and sighed. A dark five-o'clock shadow covered his chin and cheeks. "Not really. I mean, of course, there's competition out here, but no one that would want to harm my child. And, anyway, what would that do? How would that nix the competition?"

She wasn't sure.

He massaged the back of his neck then raised his head. "Wait. I didn't think anything about it at the time, but there was a hole in the fencing big enough for a pony to get its head stuck and do damage, but I caught it in time. Then a latch was broken and two horses got out, and one of my new mares got really sick. Doc said she'd eaten some poisonous berries. I searched the grazing pastures and we rode the trails. Nothing."

"We?"

"Candy and I. She's my manager."

"You think these were deliberate incidents? By whom?" Ruby asked. She made a note to talk to his manager. Get her perspective.

"I don't know, but I was thinking earlier how all these little things are adding up, cost-wise. With the unusual rain plus the extra costs, things could go south financially if it keeps up."

"Maybe that's what someone wants."

"There are three horse outfitters in the North Cascades. We all have trail rides, but I provide more amenities like picnics in the parks and moonlight rides for couples. I'm the most remote, but also the most popular when the weather's nice. I just can't believe this is happening again." He put his coffee on a side table, the steam pluming in the air.

"What is happening again? Has she been taken before?" Ruby asked and leaned forward.

Nick let out a heavy breath and rubbed his eyes with the heels of his hands. He stood and paced, his cowboy boots clicking along the pine floor. "My sister went missing when she was the exact same age as Zoe. I was eight. We lived in Seattle but hiked the mountains often and camped at Harlequin Campground."

"Did she go missing from the campground?"

"Nearby. They had a festival going on similar to what was happening today. My dad had gone to get ice-cream cones for us. My mom had gone into the bathrooms, and we were sitting outside on the bench waiting. Lizzie needed to potty, and she was only three. I didn't want her to have an accident or get in trouble for not letting her go, so I just sent her in to Mom." Nick stopped pacing and his voice grew thin. "Mom came out. Lizzie didn't."

"I'm so sorry." What an enormous amount of guilt that would have been heaped on a young boy. "Did they…? Has she ever been found?"

He shook his head. "No. Police, park rangers, the FBI—they all suspected that someone led her out the back door of the restroom. Or she wandered out on her own, but I don't think she would have done that. Plus, she knew Dad was buying a chocolate ice-cream cone for her. She never passed up ice cream. They searched for weeks. No trace. She simply vanished."

Ruby's dad had vanished from her life, but she knew he lived about fifteen miles from her until last year, when he moved to Pensacola. She didn't wonder if he was dead or alive. "How long ago was that?" She wasn't sure how old Nick was. Early thirties, if she had to guess.

"Twenty…" His eyes widened. "It'll be twenty-five years in just a few days."

His sister would have been twenty-eight years old if she was alive. One of the four candidates vying for two open slots with the PNK9 unit, Brandie Weller, was obsessed with cold cases involving young girls who'd gone missing in and around the neighboring parks because she'd gone missing as a child. She'd found five possibilities that could be her. This long-lost-sister case might be one of those five, though it was unlikely, since there was a one-year age gap between Brandie and Lizzie Rossi. She might mention it to the chief for Brandie to look into. Wouldn't hurt.

"Why did you move into the park?" His home wasn't but about ten minutes from Harlequin Campground, where his sister had gone missing. Had he been searching for her all these years? How heartbreaking. "You said you were from Seattle?"

He nodded. He stared out at the dark storm. She could tell he wasn't observing the wind and rain but was somewhere back twenty-five years ago. "I am. I left for a while. Things were difficult and I guess I wanted to run away. Went into the army. Became military police, then CID. The Criminal Investigations Division if you don't know."

"I do." That made sense. His cool composure that seemed to override his fear. His steady pacing that wasn't frantic.

"Most of our cases, sadly, were child-related or domestic abuse. Both tragic. But with every single crime against a child, all I saw was Lizzie and what could have happened to her. It was taking a toll on me and my marriage. So I didn't re-up. I came here. To be close to Lizzie, or to be around if—if by some slim chance she ever returned. I know that sounds illogical."

"I understand. I'm sorry for all you've lost. All you've seen." She'd seen some horrible things, too. She hadn't known about his military background. She'd look into that. "Let's circle back to your business. Tell me more about what you do."

"Besides being trail guides, we also have independent rides. We keep expanding with lessons and even using the stables for destination weddings. I feel blessed and so undeserving." He mumbled that last line and Ruby didn't push. He pointed toward the wall of windows and the unrelenting weather. "I don't see this letting up tonight. You're more than welcome to bunk in my guest room upstairs. I know that's probably weird, but even getting out to drive is risky. Tomorrow should be better weather."

The thought that someone might come back for Zoe gave her anxiety even though her father was former military, and a detective at that. Four eyes were better than two. She'd like to stay. "I would appreciate that, Mr. Rossi."

"Please call me Nick. Especially if I'm calling you Ruby. I noticed the accent. Where you from originally?"

"Born and raised in Mobile, Alabama. Worked in the K-9 unit and then I transferred here to join the PNK9 team four years ago. We're headquartered in Olympia, but we're all assigned to different national parks in Washington. Mine is North Cascades. I do love it here."

"That's a long way from home." He let the statement hang in case she wanted to discuss why she moved twenty-eight hundred miles away. She didn't. But he'd opened up, and she found that relating to a person helped them offer more details in a case.

"I had a bad romantic relationship, and I needed a new start."

Now she was two for two in bad romantic relationships, and her relationship with her father was nonexistent. She'd dated Jalen for two years, and unfortunately, he didn't understand that having girlfriends and flings on the side was frowned upon in committed relationships. He'd shattered her heart. She hadn't been enough for her dad—he'd walked out. And she hadn't been enough for Jalen to keep his eyes and hands from wandering on multiple occasions, and she'd been just stupid enough to believe he'd change.

She'd wanted out of Mobile. Grandmama had passed, and Mom had remarried and was happy. Had a new life. Ruby had wanted that, too. So she'd applied and gotten the job. She'd dated some, but Eli Ballard was the first man she'd had a relationship with longer than a month in the four years being here.

Pepper rubbed against her leg as if knowing her ache and Ruby scratched her ears, then removed her masking-tape lint roller from her backpack and ran it down her pant legs. She loved dogs, but the dog hair drove her up the wall. Her colleagues had gotten used to her brushing it off of herself and them. It was kind of an irritating running joke with them.

"I'm sorry to hear that. My wife passed two years ago in a car accident. Everything changed in that moment. We didn't have a perfect marriage by any means, but we had a good one. I had my fair share of rotten relationships before her, though, so I understand."

"Daddy, I'm hungry and Goldie's hungry, too." Zoe slid off the chair and entered the living room. "I want chicken nuggets."

Ruby grinned at the little cutie pie who looked very much like her father, with jet-black hair and bright blue eyes.

"It is getting close to suppertime." Nick stood. "Ruby, you hungry?"

"I could eat."

She followed him into the kitchen, Pepper on her heels, and he tossed some chicken nuggets and fries in the oven, then grinned. "I think I can do better than this for us."

"Hey, I grew up on chicken nuggets and microwaved mac and cheese. My mom worked two jobs and grandmama cleaned houses, so I was by myself a lot as a middle schooler and teenager."

"You found my daughter. I can't thank you with frozen chicken parts and crinkle cuts." He chuckled and pulled out a package of chicken breasts from the fridge and some summer vegetables.

"Can I at least help you?" she asked.

"Nah. Just relax. Tell me something else about yourself."

"Well, I went to school on a volleyball scholarship. I have an awesome serve. I run about eight miles a day and hike on weekends. I've never ridden a horse."

He paused in chopping the zucchini and squash. "Excuse me? What did you say? You've never ridden a horse? Ever?"

She laughed. "No. I'm not scared of them. I just never have."

"Zoe, can you believe Officer Ruby has never been in a saddle?" He winked at Zoe, who was slurping a juice box.

"I rides horsies all the days."

"You hear that, Ruby? All. The. Days." He laughed again. It was deep and kind. She liked hearing it. "We need to take Officer Ruby on a horse ride, don't we, punkin?"

"Yes! But not in the rain." Zoe's little face was serious.

Ruby also loved how he called her Officer Ruby to Zoe. It was cute and respectful. She wouldn't mind going on a horseback ride with Nick Rossi. But more than a horseback ride, she wanted to find out who was responsible for abducting his daughter today.

Nick and Ruby ate a simple chicken dinner with vegetables and grown-up mac and cheese—no orange powder— and talked about their lives. They didn't get too in-depth, but that was okay. Then Ruby played *Candy Land* with Zoe, and he'd enjoyed seeing his little girl laugh. He didn't hate hearing Ruby laugh, either.

Zoe didn't seem shaken up by the incident today. The abductor had told her it was a game, which kept her from having a meltdown. Nick had made it clear to Zoe it wasn't a game he ever wanted her to play again. After that, she'd been clingy until Ruby had suggested a board game and then she refused to go to bed. It was past eight now, and she was exhausted. So was Nick.

The day had taken a toll on him. To think someone might be messing with his outfitter and using his daughter as some kind of sick pawn was unthinkable and made no sense. But the fact that Zoe had been taken only days before the twenty-fifth anniversary of his sister vanishing… Who would know that? Why would they do this? He was so confused but thankful that Ruby was here working the case. She had a confidence he admired and a calming presence. If she hadn't stuck around, he might be a basket case himself.

The storm had ebbed, but not enough that Ruby could leave. She mentioned she lived in Newhalem, a small unincorporated town in the western foothills of the North Cascades. He was vaguely familiar.

"Daddy, I'm not tired." Zoe rubbed her eyes and poked out her bottom lip.

"No, I can tell." He picked her up and snuggled her against him. He loved her after-bath scent of lavender and baby powder, and her hair was still damp. "How about I read you and Goldie a story."

"Goldie wants to hear Peter Rabbit. Her wikes Peter Rabbit. And her wants Officer Ruby to read it."

"Of course, she does." He grinned at Ruby. "But Officer Ruby is busy." He didn't want to put her on the spot. She'd been a real champ playing *Candy Land* four hundred times.

"I'd be happy to." Zoe flew into her arms and Ruby carried her to the bedroom.

Nick waited a few moments then slipped into the hall to peek in on the officer and his daughter. Zoe was nestled in bed and Ruby sat beside her. "When I was a little girl, my mama tucked me in bed. Like this." She slipped the covers under Zoe's body. "Tuck. Tuck. Tuck," she said as she continued until Zoe was snug and giggling.

"I wike that. I wike you," Zoe said.

"I like you, too." She grabbed *The Tale of Peter Rabbit* and read it with inflections, and when it was over Zoe suckered her into reading the *Velveteen Rabbit*.

Finally, she was asleep, and Goldie was, too. Nick watched as Ruby studied his sleeping girl and smoothed her hair. So maternal. Soft and delicate.

"I'm going to keep you safe, little one," Ruby whispered and placed a quiet kiss on her forehead. Nick swallowed down the emotion then made a little noise to let Ruby know he was around. She saw him enter and he switched on Zoe's night-light.

"She doesn't like the dark," he said.

"No one really does."

They tiptoed from the room and Nick left the door cracked open. He still kept a monitor in his room in case she awoke or Goldie alerted him. "I'll make us some apple cider."

"Sounds good."

Once he made it, he returned to the living room. Ruby had her head back against the couch, her eyes closed. Her dark hair touched her shoulders in soft waves. Her lashes were thick and long, fanning along her skin. He hadn't been attracted to anyone since his late wife, and the sensation scared him a little. As if she felt his presence, she opened her eyes.

"Smells good." He handed her a cup and she sipped. "I keep wondering if this abduction today has anything to do with your sister's disappearance twenty-five years ago. I reached out to our technical analyst, Jasmin, while you were making cider and she's doing some research on the abduction and anyone who might have been connected to it that still lives or works in or near the park.

You need to know that. It's bound to open up some old wounds, and I'm sorry for that in advance."

"I understand." He appreciated her sensitivity. "Whatever we can do to keep Zoe safe. Do you think this woman will try again? Or that she's working alone?"

Ruby rubbed her eyes. "You said the woman who asked about the horseback riding pointed to a man and boy as her husband and son. Then she dropped her purse when you looked over at them. Correct?"

"Actually, I looked at Zoe when she dropped her purse."

"I see. Did the man and son wave or give any indication they were with the woman and were aware of what she was talking to you about?"

Nick thought back. He'd glanced as she pointed. The man wasn't looking. The boy was, but he didn't wave. "Not really."

Ruby grimaced. "It's possible she used them. When you looked at Zoe, she dumped her purse. Did you see her stumble or her purse slip?"

"No. My attention was on Zoe. I don't like taking my eyes off her." But he had. When she dropped that stupid purse. Being polite hadn't paid off today.

"That might have been a diversion, Nick. And it might mean the person who took Zoe wasn't working alone and there's an agenda." She paused. "Or it was a crime of opportunity. Maybe the woman who took Zoe had been watching. Stalking even. She saw the purse drop and your attention diverted, and she rushed in. We need to determine which scenario is correct."

"But why take her and leave her? If she wanted Zoe safe, that was a terrible place to put her. She could have fallen. If she wanted Zoe for herself, then she would have run with her and not looked back."

Ruby hovered her lips over the rim of her cup. "I wish I knew. I'd like to find the woman who asked about horseback riding. When the weather clears, I'll get a sketch artist out here to draw her. Then we can circulate her photo. If that man and boy are her family, then we can lean toward it being a crime of opportunity. If not, we have a solid lead to whoever took her and know that more than one person is in play."

They listened to the rain beat on the roof and the rumble of thunder. Flashes of lightning streaked across the windowpanes. Nick thought he heard something. He cocked his head. He had.

"The horses are whinnying. They're out. I shouldn't hear them this close to the house. In this weather. Not good." He jumped up but froze. He didn't want to leave Zoe. Especially if this was a planned attack.

Ruby noticed his trepidation and bolted for the door, swinging it open. "I got it. Pepper, stay."

"Wait!" he called, but Ruby was already running into the storm. She'd never even ridden a horse. There was no way she would know how to put them back in the gate and they were probably scared. And worse, she was alone and a threat to the kidnapper.

He ran to the front door but he couldn't see anything.

"Ruby!" he called and waited a beat. Thunder cracked the sky again.

Then he heard a blood-curdling cry.

THREE

Ruby fell a second time to the soggy ground as something hard smacked her upper back. She'd spotted two horses roaming and had begun directing them toward the pen when someone had hit her and she'd crashed into the mud the first time.

Now, on wobbly legs, she tried to stand again, rain running into her eyes and blurring the person dressed in black, hidden in shadows and unidentifiable. The figure rushed her, and she rolled onto her back, using her legs to kick the assailant away. She stood and got her balance. The attacker turned and ran. She gave chase, her feet sinking in the mud, the rain plastering her hair to her face and running cold down the inside of her shirt.

She gained on the figure. Not as tall as her, but fit and strong. As the edge of the woods materialized, she tackled the attacker, but was bucked off. Her assailant grabbed a fallen branch and swung it.

Ruby rolled out of the way and the attacker charged her again, branch raised and ready to strike. Ruby mentally kicked herself for running out without her gun. Total rookie mistake. She felt a pine cone and chucked it at the masked person, hoping for a distraction.

It worked and Ruby sprang to her feet. The attacker

rammed the branch into Ruby's torso, shoving her into a tree, the rough bark digging into her already bruised back. She hit her head on the trunk and lights spotted before her vision. The attacker rammed again, but Ruby managed to clutch the heavy branch that was riddled with pine needles. She returned the shove, knocking the person off balance.

The creep released the branch, turned and sprinted through the trees. Ruby gave chase again, stumbling over limbs, more branches and tree stumps. Thunder rumbled louder and the rain grew heavier, blinding her vision like a wet curtain. And in the thick of the forest, she lost the attacker.

She raced back to the house, and the horses were still roaming. As she approached, Nick was on the porch, eyes wide and pacing. "Ruby! I heard you scream."

"Pepper, come!" She knew she'd still be placed where she was told to be, but frantic. Pepper bounded out of the house and up to Ruby. She loved on her. "I'm okay. Is Zoe okay?"

He nodded and held up the battery-operated monitor. "Yes. Still asleep." He touched her face, which was wet and filthy. "I wanted to come out and help you but I couldn't leave Zoe alone. Are you hurt? What happened?"

She told him she was fine and skipped some of the details so as not to worry him further, or make him feel guiltier over not dashing out to help her. She was glad he hadn't. "Zoe is the number one priority. I'm a trained officer and can take care of myself. Which I did. Let's get inside."

"I need to put the horses up. Can you keep watch over Zoe?" He handed her the monitor.

"Nick, it's not a good idea to be out there alone. Whoever it was could return or still be out there. The guy was clearly luring *you*."

Nick stood on the porch, his jaw clenched. "You don't know that. What if they knew *you'd* come out. If they're after me or Zoe, they wouldn't want a federal officer too close."

Ruby had briefly thought of that, but it was a stretch. Whoever had unlatched the gate couldn't be sure who would come out to relock it, and unless they'd been outside in the storm lurking, they wouldn't know she was even inside.

But they might be watching. Stalking. Could have been for a long time.

"My horses could be in danger. I have to go." He laid a gentle hand on her shoulder. "I'll be careful. Former military. Former detective. Remember?" The warmth his hand brought sent a wave of flutters in her belly. She so did not need this kind of response to him.

She didn't like it, but she'd bolted out alone and he had training so, she remained silent as he jumped off the porch steps and jogged into the night. He gently called the horses and let out a low whistle. More soft words. The same way he talked to Zoe. A dad whose daughter was his prize possession. Ruby had only dreamed of being her dad's precious treasure. She admired Nick. She didn't blame him for helping a woman and turning his eyes away briefly. He was a good dad.

But his eyes had revealed his torment. He wasn't feeling like a good dad.

She heard the squeak of an iron gate that needed some WD-40, then a muffled cry on the monitor. Goldie barked.

Oh, no!

Ruby raced inside from the porch, praying Zoe was okay. She sprinted down the hall, past the living room, then pushed open Zoe's door, Pepper right beside her.

Goldie stood at the window and let out a low growl. Zoe sat up and rubbed her eyes. "I'm scared, Officer Ruby. Where's my daddy?"

Ruby peered out the window but didn't see anything due to the downpour, and the clouds inked out the moon and stars. She rushed to Zoe's side. "It's okay. Some horsies got loose and your daddy is getting them back inside the fencing."

"Did Daddy try to come inside my room?" Zoe asked.

"No," she said with caution. It appeared someone might have, though. Letting out the horses could have been a distraction to take Zoe again. But why take Zoe and leave her on a cliff? That felt more like a taunt or psychological torture toward Nick. Who would want to do that? He was right, a competitor might mess with the fencing and gate latches, but messing with his daughter wouldn't produce anything.

Nick entered the room, hair dripping wet, clothes soaked. "Zoe, you okay, baby?"

"Yes, Daddy. Are the horsies put up?"

"They are now." He rubbed her head, but kept some distance. Probably trying not to drip on her sheets.

"Did you try to come home in my window?" Zoe asked.

Nick squinted his eyes and cocked his head. "What do you mean?"

"Zoe heard something at her window. Goldie alerted with a bark and then growled. That's why I'm in here and she's awake."

Nick held her gaze, a silent fear passing from him to her as he put two and two together. Then he cleared his throat and turned his attention to his daughter. "No. It's probably just the storm blowing leaves or something."

"Goldie didn't wike it."

"No. I'm sure she didn't." He patted the dog's head. "Good girl, Goldie. You keep Zoe safe from storms." He left off "and bad people."

If a golden retriever was growling, it was serious. They made terrible guard dogs. Whoever entered would be more likely to get mauled by a dog tongue than teeth. But she was good to alert.

"Will you way by me?" Zoe rubbed her eyes.

"Let me get dry and then I will." He looked to Ruby. "Officer Ruby can keep you company until I get back. Okay?"

"Okay," she said and pulled her little pink sheets up to her chin. Her dark hair spilled into her face and Ruby's heart swelled. This child was so precious and in so much danger.

"Are you scared, Officer Ruby?"

"No. I'm here to keep you safe."

"And Daddy?"

"Yes, and Daddy."

Zoe snuggled in. "Can you tuck me ins again?"

Ruby loved her little way of speaking. "Yes, ma'am, I can." She did the "tuck, tuck, tuck" and Zoe's fears passed. She was going to miss this sweet child when the investigation was over.

Nick returned dry and Ruby whispered, "I'll be right back. Maybe take her to the kitchen for a glass of milk? Give me five minutes." She gave him a look that told him she wanted to snoop around Zoe's window without scaring the child.

Ruby hurried upstairs and grabbed her gun from the

locked case, and a flashlight, then rushed out the front door, the rain still coming down and soaking her skin cold. She cautiously kept to the side of the house and left her flashlight off until she reached Zoe's bedroom window. She saw the glow of her night-light inside, giving her clear vision of the empty room.

Someone could have easily been watching her. She would remind Nick to keep the shades drawn from now on. Stehekin was a very small community with less than one hundred residents, though in the peak months it grew with seasonal workers and tourists. The place was safe, like any place...until it wasn't.

She noticed indentions in the wooden sill and bottom of the window as if someone had been trying to jimmy open the window. That may be what Zoe heard. She didn't say she saw anyone, though. Under the roof's extension, Ruby spotted boot prints near the window and shined her light outward. The rain had covered up any tracks that might have been there. She used her cellphone camera and took a photo, with a flash, of the boot prints. Looked like work boots, not cowboy boots. A smaller shoe size than hers, but that wasn't saying a lot. Ruby had big feet for a woman—or at least they felt big to her. Size eleven.

After taking several photos and doing a perimeter check, she went back inside, dripping on the entryway floor. She shed her coat, shoes and socks, and spotted a towel on the bench by the door. Nick must have put it there for her. He was thoughtful. She quickly dried off, hurried upstairs to her travel bag and changed yet again, then brought her wet clothes down with hopes of finding a dryer.

She tiptoed along the hall and heard him reading a

story. Peter Rabbit again. She wondered if Zoe had ever seen the movie. Not that there was a movie theater in Stehekin. Only satellite TV. Nick's soft voice soothed even Ruby as he gave voice to the characters as he read. She heard a lamp click and he exited the room, pulling the door only halfway closed.

Noticing her clothing, he whispered, "The laundry room is off the kitchen."

"Did you close her blinds? I could easily see inside with the night-light."

He nodded and motioned for her to follow him. He opened the dryer and she tossed in her wet clothing. Then he added a dryer sheet and turned it on. "Someone tried to get my daughter again," he said soberly as they entered the kitchen. "What are we going to do?"

"For now, we need to rest. Tomorrow we'll make a game plan, and I'd like to stick around if that's okay. I can get a room at the lodge outside town—"

"No. Please, stay here. I know it might seem outside protocol but having you here and another set of eyes on Zoe… I'd be grateful."

In the short time being here, Ruby had already let Zoe Rossi wiggle her way into her heart. She wanted to be nearby. What concerned her was the possibility that if she spent a lot of time with Nick, he might end up there, too, and falling for another man while working a case was not happening.

Not now.

Not ever.

Nick had ended up sleeping on the floor next to Zoe's bed. Being in his own room was simply too far away and he'd already almost lost her once. Just like he'd lost

Lizzie. How could he have turned his eyes away? Less than thirty seconds. If that. He'd known better, and the guilt crushed his lungs. He could barely breathe and every time he'd almost drifted to sleep, he'd seen Zoe's lone shoe, or her sitting on the cliff ledge fifty feet from the lake and rocks below, which twisted and caused anxiety in his chest.

So he'd ended up on the floor, but the pain didn't leave. He should have made Lizzie wait until Mom came out, or Dad returned. But no. He'd watched her walk into the bathroom and assumed she would be fine.

Mom and Dad told him he wasn't to blame. That it made complete sense for him to do that, and Dad said he shouldn't have left Lizzie on the bench for Nick to watch. But nothing assuaged the guilt. By the time Nick hit fifteen, he'd fully retreated inside himself and barely spoke to his parents. He couldn't stand to be around them because he fully believed deep down that they blamed him. He got a part-time job and made sure he worked Lizzie's birthdays and on the anniversaries of her disappearance. It was too much to watch them cry and see Mom bake her favorite cake only to have it go uneaten for the most part.

He should have made her wait.

Now someone was trying to take his daughter. During his sleepless night, he'd wracked his brain, but no one came to mind. No one seemed that merciless. That heartless. That cold and cruel. Not here in Stehekin. They were community. Family.

Now, he stood at the stove, whisking pancake batter, and he turned down the burner so the bacon wouldn't burn. Might as well feed the officer who had rescued his daughter and risked her life to help him get his horses back to safety. He admired her fearlessness and the soft looks she gave Zoe. He didn't know a lot about her but she didn't wear a ring. She never mentioned having kids… unless the dog counted. Those two were inseparable. He checked his watch. Not quite 8:00 a.m.

The storm passed, leaving limbs and branches all over the property and the ground spongy, but the sky was blue right now and the sun bright. A knock sounded on the door, and he headed for it. His stable manager, Candy, stood on the other side of the glass. "Did you smell the bacon from your place?" he asked.

She snorted and entered. "No. Just wanted to stop by on my way to the stables and check in on Zoe. It's the talk of the town. Everyone is worried. Even Luca Hattaway." She gave him a knowing eye.

"Who's Luca Hattaway?" Ruby asked as she entered the living room in her dry PNK9 uniform. She looked good in it.

Candy's eyebrows rose. "Hello."

"Hi." Ruby closed the distance and held out her hand. "I'm Officer Orton with the Pacific Northwest K-9 unit. This is my partner, Pepper."

Candy grinned at the dog. "Candy Reynolds. I work for Nick. Just came by to check in on Zoe. And Luca Hattaway is the owner of Lake Chelan Stables."

"Zoe is still asleep," Nick said. "I'm making breakfast if you want to stick around." He headed back to the kitchen and began pouring batter on the griddle. "You like pancakes and bacon, Ruby?"

"Again, like I like breathing." She helped herself to a cup of coffee.

Candy stayed near the front door. "I can't stay. And I already had a protein shake."

"Suit yourself. You should know the horses were let

out last night." The last thing he wanted was Candy to get hurt. "Keep someone else with you. Don't be in the stables alone. I don't know what this person is up to, and I want everyone safe."

"Sure thing, Nick. You think all of us at Cascades Stables are in danger?" Her blue eyes revealed a measure of fear.

Nick looked to Ruby. He wasn't sure.

Ruby held her coffee mug between both hands. "We don't want to take any chances. Being in the right place at the wrong time could get you hurt, so precaution is necessary until we figure out exactly what is going on and who the target is and why."

Candy nodded and glanced back at the front door. "Joe's at the stable so I'll get going. We had several families extend their trail rides today since the weather was so nasty yesterday."

"I talked to Joe this morning. Let him know, too."

"Actually, before you go," Ruby said, "I'd like to talk to you about competitors or anyone—in particular a woman—hanging around the stables or getting close to Zoe. Like this Luca Hattaway. Seems there's bad blood there. I talked to Nick already, but I'd like an employee's perspective."

Candy's lips twisted to the side and she inhaled. "Our competitors are Lake Chelan Stables, Evergreen Outfitters and Pacific Northwest Trails. We know them well enough. Luca is a jerk, but I don't see him trying to hurt Zoe or Nick."

"Any animosity? Employees circulating from one establishment to the next?" Ruby asked.

"Jeremy Benedict worked as a prime tour guide at Evergreen, then came to us because of better pay. He was great, but…"

"But?"

Nick swallowed the last of his orange juice. "But we had a difference in opinion on which trails to take advanced riders on. He was a bit of a thrill seeker and I have to think about liability. He didn't like not having a say and left us for Pacific Northwest, but rumor has it the same thing happened and he's now at Lake Chelan Stables."

"Working for Luca Hattaway?" Ruby asked.

"Yes."

Candy frowned. "He just likes to be in charge. He's a great guy and a great tour guide. I don't see him being involved in a kidnapping." Candy cast a wary glance at Nick. "But Yolanda Martin left us upset about six months ago and went to Lake Chelan as well. I hear she loves to talk trash about us."

"Does Zoe know Yolanda?" Ruby asked.

Nick nodded. "She does, but barely. I'm not sure she'd recognize her. She's only seen her a few times."

"Why did she leave?" Ruby sipped her coffee and Nick added more pancakes to the griddle and removed the bacon from the grease popping in the pan.

"You go ahead and make a plate. No point in them getting cold."

Ruby snagged a plate on the island and helped herself to two pancakes and two pieces of bacon, then sat at the bar stool, slathering butter on the pancakes and pouring on warm maple syrup.

"Yolanda had a thing for Nick. Nick politely put her in her place, but she didn't get the hint. She came on pretty strong and he let her go when she didn't respond well."

Candy picked up a piece of bacon and grinned. "You just can't turn down bacon."

Ruby chuckled and indulged in a bite of pancakes. "How did she respond?"

"Keyed his car. Joe caught her."

Nick groaned. "Yolanda is twenty-two. She'd just gone through a bad breakup, and I was being nice. She took it wrong. Very wrong."

"Obsessively wrong," Candy said.

Nick narrowed his gaze at Candy. He wouldn't say obsessive. Maybe irrational. "But I don't think she'd kidnap Zoe. She has no motive." Nick turned off the griddle and rinsed the batter bowl.

"Have you heard from her since she left that day?" Ruby asked and dipped her bacon in her syrup.

Nick's neck heated and he felt it spread to his cheeks. "I have, actually."

"You didn't tell me that." Candy scoffed and folded her arms over her chest.

Nick didn't have to tell Candy everything and certainly not personal stuff. "She texted me a few times to apologize and ask for her job back. To which I said no. She asked if we could get together and talk about it. Nothing romantic." He sighed. "I declined."

Ruby pushed aside her plate and tented her fingers on the counter. "Do you still have those texts?"

Nick piled pancakes on his plate, though he had zero appetite. But he knew he needed to eat. "I think so." He grabbed his phone off the counter and scrolled through it. "Yeah." He handed her the phone. Ruby read through the texts.

"You said there were no hard feelings and nothing to discuss, and, anyway, you had promised to take Zoe to the park. She said that was too bad. Maybe another time. You didn't respond." Ruby's eyes narrowed. "I'd like to have our tech expert look into her. See if she's had any charges against her, restraining orders or even complaints from other employers. You have anyone else that might fit the bill? Anyone who might hold a grudge against you for something?"

"I do thorough background checks on employees," Nick said. "I can tell you she's had no priors other than a couple of speeding tickets in Seattle. Her references were impeccable."

"Still. Grudges? Anyone? Tell me more about Luca Hattaway."

"We argued a little when we bid on the same horse and I outbid him. He was pretty upset but surely not enough to do this."

"I want to question all your rivals, and Yolanda Martin and Jeremy Benedict. He might have nursed a grudge."

Candy snagged one more piece of bacon. "I should get going."

Nick walked her to the door and locked it behind her. He returned to the kitchen and the pile of uneaten pancakes, enough for an army. He'd freeze the leftovers and microwave them for quick breakfasts for Zoe.

"How did you sleep?" Ruby asked.

"I didn't. I stayed in Zoe's room." He checked the time on the stove clock. "She should be waking soon. She's always been a good sleeper and I know yesterday wore her out." Had worn him out, too. "How did you sleep?"

"I'm used to staying in foreign places. Sometimes the job calls for it, so I slept well. Thanks." She carried her empty plate to the sink.

"I can get that," he said and reached for the plate,

brushing his hand against hers and being taken aback by how it felt. Soft and sizzling.

She paused, held his gaze, then swallowed hard. "I can help. Least I can do."

"Okay," he said and stepped back. Why in the world had her touch felt like that? He shouldn't be feeling anything but guilt for almost losing Zoe and fear over what might happen next. Zoe alone was his priority. No romantic involvement. He couldn't, and wouldn't, let anything or anyone distract him from his daughter again. And a romantic entanglement would definitely do that.

She rinsed the plate and loaded it in the empty dishwasher.

"Daddy, I'm awake, and Goldie, too." Zoe padded into the kitchen, sleepy-eyed and with her hair tousled.

"I see this." He scooped her up and kissed her warm cheek, which had a line from her pillow. "I made pancakes and bacon."

"I wuv pancakes. Officer Ruby, do you wuv pancakes?" she asked as she peeped over his shoulder at Ruby.

"I certainly do. I had two of them."

"I want two of them, too."

"You got it."

They would be going to church in two hours and the day would be filled with fun for Zoe; he was going to see to it. He strode into the living room to grab the remote and turn on some worship music when glass shattered the living-room window and a bullet slammed into the fireplace mantel, knocking a family photo onto the floor.

"Get down!" Ruby hollered and grabbed her gun. "Into the inner bathroom in the hall. I've got Zoe."

Another shot slammed into the side of the other living-room window. Zoe squealed and Goldie whimpered.

Ruby cradled his daughter and they met in the hallway. "Stay in here with Zoe."

"You don't need to be a hero, Ruby. You have no backup. Stay with us."

"Call nine-one-one." She ignored his pleas and bolted down the hall, Pepper on her heels. Once again, Nick didn't want to leave Zoe alone with a shooter outside.

All he could do was pray and hope Ruby wouldn't be hurt...or worse.

FOUR

Ruby's heart thumped wildly inside her chest as she raced out the door. She took cover behind the rocking chairs on the porch and stayed low against the side of the house. The shooter had to be in the woods. Why would someone who wanted to kidnap a child be shooting with the child in the house?

Her thoughts raced as she tried to concoct a plan to get into the woods without being an open target, but there wasn't a way. She had no cover once she left the house. The shooter likely knew that.

A bullet slammed above her head and she shrieked and ducked, then used her sat phone to call her colleagues, who were still at the ranger station. Tanner answered on the first ring.

"How'd you sleep?" he asked.

"No time for pleasantries. The house is under fire. I repeat, the house is under fire. Need backup. ASAP."

"Roger that. Are you in the line of fire or in a safe zone?"

"Line of fire. Mr. Rossi and his daughter are inside and hopefully safe in the hall bathroom. I told him to call nine-one-one."

"Hold steady. We're on our way."

Ruby would do the best she could with the crummy conditions and hoped he and Dylan would arrive soon. They'd have to chopper in if they wanted to be fast. Ruby returned fire into the forest. There were no hiking trails on Nick's private property and the horse stables where tourists visited for riding trails and lessons were on the west side of the property. She needed the shooter to know she was armed and unafraid to fight back.

Even if she had all sorts of nervous energy, she'd been trained and had experience. She wasn't one to crack under pressure. Pepper hunkered down beside her and gave her an additional measure of comfort.

In the distance, helicopter blades whirred, which brought down her stress level. Dylan and Tanner were on their way to help. The firing stopped. If the shooter was smart, they'd recognize the contracted helicopter used by the North Cascades park rangers and know they were coming to give backup.

Wind nearly blew her against the house as the power of the blades came closer and the pilot landed. Dylan and Tanner jumped out and their K-9s ran alongside them. Then the pilot went up into the air and flew over the woods. Hopefully, the pilot would spot the shooter if he hadn't already.

"You think it's the abductor or whoever attacked you from last night?" Tanner asked. Ruby had called them after the debacle.

"I do. I just don't understand the shooting now and hiding the child to be easily found yesterday." Ruby wished she could think like a killer, but this whole thing was odd.

"Then we're going to track," Tanner said and gave the

command for his dog to track the same scent of the abductor as yesterday. He and Britta raced across the yard.

"I'll go as backup in case it gets hairy. You good here?" Dylan asked and patted his Saint Bernard.

"Yeah. Thanks."

"We can fly out, by the way. Weather is all clear today." He tossed out a command and they sprinted across the yard toward the tree line. Ruby rushed inside. She wasn't ready to leave. She was in charge of this investigation and it was clearly escalating. She needed to see this through, especially since a small child was involved.

"Nick," she called as she ran toward the bathroom in the narrow downstairs hall.

The door opened and he appeared, concern in his eyes and worry lining his brow. Zoe sat inside the bathtub with Goldie, reading a book about a giant earthworm. "I'm taking a bath without water, Officer Ruby." She grinned, clearly unaware of the danger. Nick did a good job of protecting and shielding her from fear.

But no one was shielding him at the moment and his pale face did a number on her heart. "Are you okay?" he asked with a lowered voice to keep his splashing daughter from hearing. "I know it's your job to do that kind of thing and you're more than capable, but quite frankly—and especially with my hands tied—it scared me half to death."

It wasn't his male pride talking and she appreciated that. "I certainly don't mean to scare anyone. Officer Ford is here and he and his dog are tracking the abductor's scent. If it's the same person, Britta will alert him. Officer Jeong is backing him up. The weather is clear to fly out, but since this is my case, I'll be staying in Stehekin. I need to see about lodging, and since shots were fired,

I'm suggesting that you and Zoe find lodging elsewhere, too." Though she didn't love the idea. "Do you have anywhere to stay remotely?" If they got a room at a lodge, it could bring danger to others. They couldn't be sure how brazen this person was. "Or a place to send Zoe?"

"I don't." He shrugged. "And I don't mean to sound insensitive or stubborn, but stress and anxiety can trigger epileptic seizures. Sending her away will do just that. Zoe's been seizure-free for five months. I was worried all night she'd have one, but she hasn't—she thought the gunfire was thunder. But I need her to stick to her routine and feel safe. And if this sicko is after her, then no one she's with is safe. So sending her to my parents or anyone else is out."

Ruby nodded with understanding then looked past the hallway. "Well, none of us can stay here right now. Glass is everywhere. I know a glass company in Seattle. I can call them. Unless you know of anyone closer." It'd take them two hours to arrive at the park and then they'd have to fly or ferry in, which was a four-hour trip.

"That would be great," he mumbled as he raked his hand through his hair. "I do know a guy who can board the windows until the glass company can get someone in here to measure. He has a crew who can do the clean up, too."

"Daddy, can I come out of the bathtub now? Goldie wants to come out, too."

Ruby grinned and glanced back toward the front door, where she'd commanded Pepper to stay. Too much glass for her to be inside.

"Sure, baby, and then we're going to ride horsies. Sound fun?" Nick turned to Ruby and lowered his voice. "I have to get her out of the house. Might as well take her to the stables and let her ride a little inside the indoor area."

"Once this is cleaned up, we can reevaluate what we need to do. But something's occurred to me. We have been in the kitchen all morning and it was only when you went into the living room that shots were fired."

"Far away from Zoe, who was in the kitchen."

She nodded. "Exactly. Someone wants you dead... and me. I'm a threat and an obstacle keeping this person from getting what they really want."

Nick balled a fist. "My daughter," he whispered through a hoarse voice. "But why not take her yesterday? Why put her on that ledge? Thank our Good Lord that she was left behind."

Ruby was still pondering that angle. "Someone is toying with you, or it's possible they got spooked, encountered someone and bowed out...this time. Either way, we can be sure that someone wants Zoe. And wants you dead."

"So much for my quiet Sunday morning before church." Nick huffed. "I'm not going to let anyone take my daughter." His voice was strong and resolute. Ruby wished she'd had a male protector like Nick in her own life. "Make no mistake about that."

Ruby's satellite phone rang as she walked out to get Pepper, and she hoped it was news from Tanner on the shooter, but it was the chief, Donovan Fanelli. "Hey, Chief."

"Just checking in. You holding down the fort okay?"

"Yeah. Tanner and Dylan are tracking the shooter. I assume you've heard from one of them."

"Tanner. As of now, he's still on the scent."

Good.

"I wanted to make sure you're okay. We've got enough to deal with. Mara is still in hiding and some of the team are following up on the double homicide and the latest leads. The bloodhound puppies are still missing, too."

"I know." When it rained it poured, like her mama always said, and it had been pouring down buckets over the PNK9 team these past few months. "But we've faced bad things before. Hey, while I have you on the phone, I found out that Nick Rossi's little sister went missing almost twenty-five years ago. She was three at the time. She was taken from this area." Ruby quickly filled in the chief on what she knew about Brandie Weller, the PNK9 candidate who believed she herself had been abducted from a Washington park as a toddler, and had narrowed down five cold cases of little girls who went missing that could be her.

"There's a year gap in ages between Brandie and Nick's sister, though," he said.

"I know. But it's worth letting her know."

"I agree. You need some extra hands, anyway. I'll send you Brandie and while she's helping you, she can also look into the cold case. But, Ruby, you stay on the present investigation. And when you need Brandie, you let her know that her personal quest takes the back burner."

"Thanks, Chief. But is she available to come down here?"

"She's got some time off from the Emeryton PD, where she currently works as a K-9 officer. She has an almost four-hour drive to North Cascades."

"And she's good after the incident?" Not long ago, Brandie had almost been hit by a vehicle after being deliberately pushed into oncoming traffic, and while she was dedicated to becoming a member of their elite group, nearly being killed was tough on someone, no matter what their career.

"She is. And I'm also sending Parker Walsh to help you out."

Ruby's stomach sank. Parker, another candidate for one of the open slots with PNK9, was cocky and a suspect in not only pushing Brandie into that oncoming traffic, but also other acts of sabotage against the competitors. Of the four, three had been messed with. Only Parker hadn't been a victim. Which cast him in a guilty light.

"Chief…"

"Ruby, we have no definitive proof, and he's on probation." She trusted Donovan Fanelli with her life so if he felt comfortable sending Parker, then she'd get on board. "Keep a watch. Go with your gut."

Her gut said it was a bad idea. "Roger that." She hung up and scanned the property from the broken windows. The wind had cooled the house. While she was thinking of it, she called the Seattle glass company to come measure for the new custom windows.

She returned to the hall and spotted Nick in Zoe's room packing a bag for the day.

"I'm gonna ride horses. You want to ride with me?" Zoe asked as she entered the room.

Ruby's heart reached out to the child. "I wish I could. But not today. I have a lot of work to do."

"'Cause that thunder that came through the windows?" Zoe let her daddy tie her pink tennis shoes. Innocence at its finest.

"'Cause the windows." She didn't want to lie but she also didn't want to terrify the child. She'd already been through enough in the past twenty-four hours. "But maybe another day."

Nick grinned and she noticed for the first time a dimple creasing one cheek, giving him a boyish charm. Her belly corkscrewed. How could she have this kind of reaction only weeks after breaking it off with Eli? After thinking he could be the one? Was she fickle, like her father? That thought horrified her and her chest constricted.

She could not be like her walk-away dad.

Nick had called his pastor before they left for the stables and before church started to ask for prayer and to let him know why he wouldn't be there this morning. He was thankful for his small community of believers who prayed for him and Zoe. Pastor John had offered to send over help to clean up, using the same crew he was going to call. They would have them boarded up before they arrived home later, but it would take about three weeks to get new windows installed since they were custom. As long as they were safe, he'd take boarded windows and less sunlight streaming through the house.

Zoe seemed settled but also a bit jumpy and Goldie had been sniffing the air more often. Nick feared a seizure at any moment. Why would someone set their sights on his daughter? Was it coincidence, or did it have a connection to his sister's disappearance twenty-five years ago? Ruby wasn't sure and neither was he.

She sat beside him quietly, but her eyes were alert and watchful. Her Lab sat in the back seat. She and Goldie sandwiched Zoe like pillars of protection.

Nick parked next to Candy and Joe outside the small cabin he used as an office. A few out-of-towners had chosen to keep their vehicles near the stables. "You ready to ride?" Nick asked Zoe.

"Yep. And Ruby, too."

"Not today, remember?" he asked and stepped out of the car, cautiously surveying the surroundings. Ruby was already out and doing the same, with Pepper beside her.

He unbuckled Zoe from her car seat and Goldie hopped out. Candy headed for them, waving, but her smile was shaky. He hated this for everyone.

"Hey, Zoe-girl! You ready to ride Maple?"

"Yay!" Zoe squealed and ran right into Candy's arms. Candy glanced at Nick and nodded once, letting him know through unspoken conversation that she would take care of her and keep her safe inside the arena.

"I'm going to do a sweep of the perimeter just to be safe." Ruby's phone rang and she answered. A grim expression crossed her face. She looked at Nick and shook her head.

They'd lost the shooter.

"But it was the same scent, so we can conclude that the same person who abducted Zoe Rossi also tried to shoot her father," she said into the phone.

Nick's stomach turned. Never in a million years would he have guessed something like this would happen to him…again.

Ruby nodded. "Meet me at Mr. Rossi's around lunchtime. Chief is sending Brandie and Parker in…Yeah, we already had that conversation…Oh…Okay, good deal. Can you be there in twenty minutes?…Good." She ended the call. "Two others are coming to aid in the investigation and our colleague Dylan has left to fly them in. I'll go over our game plan when they get here."

"Hopefully the house will be swept clean and boarded up by then." He hoped. "If it's not, we can meet in my office." He pointed to the old cabin. "It's roomier than it looks on the outside."

"That sounds like a good plan. I guess you picked up the fact that the dogs lost the scent. But the good news is, it's the same person."

"None of this makes sense."

"Once we're able to ask more questions and look into the past, we'll know more. I have our tech analyst, Jasmin, on it. She's looking into your sister's abduction case from twenty-five years ago. We'll want to talk to your parents."

"I'd prefer not to involve them, Ruby. Bringing it up. I know it's already on their minds with the date approaching. Still."

"They might know or remember things you don't. You were only eight, right?"

"Right." His throat burned. Dredging up the past seemed futile. He tried to avoid talking to them, especially around this time of the year. It was too hard. Too much. For all of them. He wished they had more of a relationship—with him and with Zoe—but the past couldn't be changed.

Uncertainty nearly killed him. It had aged his parents within a year of his sister vanishing. Dad's hair had gone stark white. Mom's wrinkles were pronounced and the light in her eyes had disappeared. She'd barely gotten out of bed most days and Nick fended for himself for meals and to get himself up and onto the school bus.

Life had forever changed after Lizzie disappeared.

He could not go through this again.

"Let me tag along with you to check the place out. You said you were going to do a perimeter sweep, right? I know this park, this area, like the back of my hand."

Ruby grimaced. "You're a civilian, Nick."

"I know." He rubbed his chin. "But you know my background. Do a check."

She heaved a breath through her nose.

"Ruby. Let me help you, please."

She kicked at the grass. "If anything went sideways it's me losing my job and you possibly losing your life."

He understood her position. Truly. But this was his life. "I know this terrain. I know the people you're going to interview. Someone is after my kid and trying to kill me. Don't let me sit on my hands. I can't. I won't." He didn't want to throw an ultimatum at her. But he wasn't going to sit idly by.

Finally, she nodded. "Fine. But so you know, I am going to do a background check on you."

"You'll like what you find," he teased.

"Don't get cocky. It's not attractive." Her grin revealed she'd picked up on his humor and realized that he wasn't being arrogant. But she would like what she found. Nick had been a good detective. And at times, missed it.

"My apologies." He took her hand, feeling the softness of her fingertips and suddenly wishing he hadn't touched her. He swallowed hard. "Thank you. I know you're sticking your neck out for me."

She blinked a few times, not looking him in the eye, and he wondered if she had felt the same connection he had. She gently removed her hand from his and tucked a hair behind her ear. "I am and I appreciate that you recognize it. Now, let's do that perimeter sweep."

He removed his Glock from his ankle. "I really do have a concealed-carry permit. It's all legal."

"I believe you." She tossed him a playful look. "Still gonna check."

He chuckled again as they started north of the stables.

"You mentioned why you ended up here, but why running a horse outfitter?" Ruby asked. "Just curious."

"My wife, Penelope, whom I'd met and married while stationed at Fort Bragg in North Carolina, thought it might be best not to re-up when my contract was done and suggested the business since her family owned an outfitter like ours here in the Appalachian Mountains. But I didn't want to stay in North Carolina. The Cascades called to me. The thought that Lizzie might resurface and I wasn't there drove me crazy. When Penelope told me that she was pregnant with Zoe, it sealed my decision and we moved. Came here to the park." He surveyed the area. Nothing out of the ordinary. "Let's check the shed."

She nodded once. "Ever consider going back into it?"

"I'm a single dad. I keep the hours I want here." Maybe when Zoe was older he'd think about going into law enforcement again.

They approached the shed and Ruby took the lead. "No locks?"

"There should be. But there's nothing of any value and we never use it. I'm right behind you."

She swung open the door and aimed her gun. It was dark inside—cobwebs abounded—and it was full of old equipment and saddles. Ruby cleared the shed as he backed her up. She glanced down.

"Those are footprints in the dust."

She took out her cell phone and took a few photos.

Nick examined the prints himself. They were fresh.

Someone had been inside his shed.

The question was…why?

FIVE

Ruby entered the office behind Nick, Pepper at her side. They'd finished securing the perimeter and making the inside of the stable as safe as possible for Zoe. She'd been riding for about an hour. According to Nick, she never tired. It did look like fun.

They'd discussed the footprints and concluded that someone was using the shed to hide out. Nick said nothing inside was of any value and nothing appeared to have been stolen. Nick had put a padlock on it. They talked ideas and theories for a while and Nick put Zoe down for a nap in his stable office after her lunch. After she woke, Candy stopped by to take Zoe to the stables while Nick was meeting the rest of the team.

Now, he scooped coffee into a filter while she sat in a brown club chair in the small conference room of the cabin's office. It was a place where he talked with clients to help them plan tours and vacation adventures. Ruby checked her watch, then heard vehicles. The rest of the team had arrived.

She stood and went to the front door. Tanner Ford and Dylan Jeong, with their K-9s, led the pack. Behind them were the two candidates the chief had sent: Brandie

Weller and Parker Walsh with their German shepherds, Taz and Rosie. Ruby motioned them all into the conference room and they squeezed in, their dogs sitting at attention at their feet.

Ruby reintroduced Tanner and Dylan to Nick, then she pointed to the two PNK9 candidates and briefly explained that they'd be helping out. She hoped Parker had been telling the truth and he was innocent.

Brandie and Parker both shook hands with Nick, and while Brandie sat at the table with the rest of them, Parker chose a club chair a few feet away with Rosie at his feet.

"Parker, come sit with us. It'll be easier to talk." Was he singling himself out because he thought he was too good, or because he felt ostracized? If he was innocent, Ruby didn't want to be a part in shaming him. He deserved a fair shot until they knew for sure if he was causing trouble among the three other candidates. If not, another of them was.

As Parker joined them, Ruby briefed the team and Tanner brought them up to speed on losing the shooter in the woods.

Now it was time to form a game plan. Ruby stood and pointed to the whiteboard in the corner. "Can I use that?"

"Sure. Let me grab you a dry-erase marker and eraser." Nick hurried from the room and returned, handing her a blue marker and eraser.

"We're going to divide and conquer," Ruby said. "The faster we move, hopefully, the faster we'll catch the suspect." But they all knew it wasn't that easy. They'd been looking for Mara Gilmore and following the stolen-puppy leads for a few months. Nothing was fast. Not like in movies and books. Time eked by when it came to investigative work.

"Tanner and Parker, you two cover the rival companies. Lake Chelan. Specifically, Luca Hattaway, who was outbid on the same horse and sore about it. Also, Yolanda Martin." She detailed the woman's obsession with Nick, noticing his neck turn red, and read the text messages sent six months ago after she'd been fired. "The other rivals include Evergreen Outfitters and Pacific Northwest Trails. Jeremy Benedict has worked here and Evergreen and is now at Lake Chelan. He didn't like not being in charge. Question him. Question everyone."

"Got it," Tanner said. Parker nodded his agreement.

"Dylan, you and Brandie talk to employees here when they come in from tours—until then, Brandie, you can work the cold cases. Nick only has four, but they might know something or feel comfortable voicing thoughts without Nick around. Use Ridge." Dylan's Saint Bernard did have the shooter's scent already. "Talk to people working the Lake Chelan ferry and see if there's anyone who was on it in the past week who can connect with Nick." At their nods, she continued, "Nick and I will talk to friends and neighbors and comb the park. It's possible more than one child was targeted. We just can't be sure of anything right now. Any theories?"

"I did a background on you, Mr. Rossi," Tanner said. "Saw you're former military. Could someone be trying to kill you or could the kidnapping be some kind of vendetta from your CID days? You put anyone away that had kids? Hurt kids? Anyone holding a grudge?"

Excellent questions. Leave it to Tanner to do the background. Though he hadn't told her he'd done it, and she was the lead on this case. Did he think she had poor judgment because of her choice in boyfriends? Eli might be a very bad man—he *was* connected to the double homicide of his business partner and her boyfriend. There was a possibility he was innocent, but a slim possibility.

She hadn't voiced that the last time the team had met via video call to discuss Eli and the follow-up. They'd only think her emotions were getting in the way. And maybe they were. After all, allowing a civilian to help with this investigation went against her better judgment.

Nick cleared his throat. "We all make enemies, I suppose, in law enforcement. Sadly, most of our CID cases are crimes against children and assaults on women. I saw stuff I can't unsee."

Which was why he ended up leaving CID. Ruby had been surprised at his transparency and how easily it had come. No one she'd ever dated before had ever been that personal.

"I understand," Ruby said. "Those crimes are the toughest to me, too. You need to really think about it and check out cases where anyone incarcerated at your hand was recently released. Make a call. Do what you need to."

Nick nodded. "I can do that right now, unless you need me for anything else."

Ruby shook her head. "Go ahead. We're just going to finish up." Nick slipped from the room. "Anyone else have any comments, suggestions?"

Tanner spoke up. "I ran his background because I couldn't sleep last night. I had planned to fill you in, but we got called while you were in the line of fire. I don't want you to think I've overstepped my bounds. I trust you, Ruby."

She needed to hear that. And she suspected Tanner knew it, too. "Thank you. Nick did tell me earlier that he was former army. Criminal Investigations Division. We have new angles now. Someone is targeting his daughter and this person knows that his sister's twenty-fifth anniversary of going missing is coming up. That's not private knowledge."

"I'll be digging deeper into the five little girls that went missing around twenty-three to twenty-five years ago," Brandie said. "Jasmin and I are going to work on this angle and see if anyone from Mr. Rossi's past might have resurfaced. I don't think I'm Lizzie Rossi. The age is off, but I'd prefer not to even mention to Mr. Rossi that it's a thin possibility. I've had a lot of false leads before and given families false hope. I don't want to be wrong again."

It was no longer a secret anymore that Brandie thought she might have been abducted when she was a small child. She said she had fuzzy memories that didn't make sense. And when her parents died in an accident last year, she discovered strange papers in the attic—a few ancient-looking attempts at creating an authentic birth certificate, plus brochures of several national parks in the Pacific Northwest. That discovery, coupled with their cagey behavior and moving every couple of years, insisting on homeschooling her when she wanted to go to public school and the lack of photographs of her before she was a teenager, had made Brandie suspicious. She'd looked into their pasts and discovered they had no backgrounds before she was a young child. Given this and her strange recurring dreams about a park and someone picking her up and running with her in a crowd had made her wonder if she could have been kidnapped by her parents as a toddler. Ruby certainly understood why she thought so.

"We'll keep it quiet. In the meantime, as you're researching the case, make calls. Including his parents. He doesn't want it brought up with the anniversary approaching but we don't have a choice. He knows this. Be discreet. Anyone who may have been around at that time—family, family friends who moved right after or right before the abduction. Cover every angle." She knew Brandie would. She was meticulous and wouldn't leave any stone unturned. Ruby only had her for three days. She'd make the most of the time.

"I'm on it."

"There's a lodge about a mile away for rooms. Brandie you can take your pick. Lodge or you can bunk in my queen bed at Nick's."

Brandie grinned. "I appreciate the offer, but I'd prefer the lodge since what I'm working on is sensitive."

Good call. "Okay. I'll have Jasmin handle the lodging. Parker, you can bunk with Dylan. Tanner's on his own. Cool?" Tanner was a lone wolf and liked his privacy so she wouldn't ask him to be a bunk mate. He'd say no, anyway. Dylan, while a thrill seeker, would keep an eye on Parker. Until they knew for certain what was going on, Parker was getting a babysitter.

Parker's jaw twitched. If he was innocent, she was sorry, but if he wasn't, then all precautions were necessary.

"Cool," Dylan said and punched Parker's shoulder. "Ridge snores."

"Great."

Nick reentered the conference room. "I made that call you asked me to. To see if anyone I had a hand in putting away was released. I have a small list. One name in particular gives me pause."

"Why's that?" Ruby asked.

"Because I called all the parole officers and he's the only one who hasn't shown up for his last check-in."

* * *

Nick was reeling over the news and his stomach had sunk like a weighted brick in his gut. He never dreamed this nightmare might actually be a vendetta against him. The guilt it brought was another heavy layer of concrete over his heart. "His name is Aaron Millsap. Twenty-four now. He was the grown son of a soldier deployed. Lived at Fort Bragg with his mom and two younger brothers. But the neighbor's daughter claims he tried to shove her in a car and abduct her. She had bruises on her arms and face where she said he hit her. She'd just turned thirteen. He claimed innocence, but the evidence against him was insurmountable and solid. A neighbor's security camera caught him—though the hit to the face happened prior and wasn't on footage. His defense was they were just messing around. Weak. The bruises were accidental but not intentional. He wasn't roughhousing her. But he was. He went away on attempted kidnapping with intent to harm. He was sentenced to five years. Served three."

Ruby folded her arms over her head. "No one knows where he is? No paper trail?"

"Not according to the officers I've talked with. Family says they have no idea, but he had a girlfriend. She sent him letters in prison. She might be footing his bill to go underground." And she might be the woman who lured Zoe into the woods.

"Now that Zoe has had some time to decompress," Ruby said, "I'd like to bring in a friend and fellow PNK9 agent to talk to her."

"Jacqueline?" Tanner asked.

Ruby nodded. "Jacqueline Gomez is excellent with kids. A gift. She has psychology and nursing degrees and she was also in the army. One of our best. If anyone can coax a reliable description from Zoe, it'll be Jacqueline, and she'll know if she's pushing too hard. Would you agree to that?"

Nick would agree to almost anything if it meant finding who had taken Zoe and tried to kill him. And who'd tried to beat up Ruby, too. "Yes. I'll agree."

"Great. She'll be coming in from the Mount Rainier area. So it'll be later today or maybe in the morning, depending on her cases. I'll call her. Anything else?"

No one had questions. Assignments were tasked and Ruby had commanded the team like a well-oiled machine. He liked her calm demeanor and confident air. It gave him hope she'd find Zoe's kidnapper. Everyone was dismissed, and he hung back with Ruby.

"How comfortable do you feel leaving Zoe with Candy while we investigate?" Ruby asked.

"Not very. Not that I don't trust Candy. I do. I just trust me more." Or did he? He tried not to second-guess himself, but he'd turned his back for ten seconds and she was gone. Leaving the premises might be detrimental to her, though, and cause seizures. He needed his head in the game. Put on his old investigator hat and get the job done, connect the dots. But he couldn't stop fixating on Zoe and what might have happened if she hadn't been on that ledge.

"I'll see if they can send one of our SUVs in on a barge with Jacqueline," Ruby said glancing around at her team. "I need a vehicle, too." She sighed. "Until then, I'll do preliminary work until she gets here. Make phone calls. Dig. Can we use your office?"

"Absolutely."

"This evening we'll get started on foot. So you know, I'd love to be the one to be on Zoe's protection detail instead of Jacqueline. I loved tucking her in and reading her books. She's a real doll, Nick. You've done a great job as a dad. But I can't fully investigate and be on protection detail. I need to be out there in the field since I'm the lead investigator."

Nick squeezed her arm. "Ruby, I don't think you're trying to pass the buck on watching my daughter. I want to help you find her abductor. I have skills to help you. So if you need to bring in someone else, I trust you."

Ruby seemed relieved and her shoulders relaxed. "Jacqueline can keep Zoe safe when we're investigating, and with her medical background and K-9 training, you can be sure she's protected all around. Plus, her German shepherd, Jesse, is cross-trained in suspect apprehension, odor detection and protection. Which means he has a sharp bite." She grinned and he laughed.

"Good to know." He was thankful Ruby wasn't going off alone. She was capable and fully trained, but she might be a direct target now, too, since she wasn't leaving. She was a threat. An obstacle to the plan. She needed someone watching her back. Besides Pepper, who never left her side. Even now she sat with her tongue lolling. And he wanted to help, wanted to be her backup. "I'll make coffee and you can do what you need in the conference room. If you need supplies, I can get them."

"Great. Thanks." Her gaze lingered on his and then she broke contact and headed back inside the cabin.

Yep, he'd felt that zinger. Wished he hadn't.

He went into the indoor arena where they gave lessons and stood at the entrance, watching Zoe on Maple. Riding with a big smile. She was always happiest after a nap. Goldie walked beside the horse. Man, that dog loved her.

And he loved that dog. Candy led by the reins, talking to Zoe, but Nick couldn't hear what she said.

Zoe spotted him. Her smile lit up his heart like a Christmas tree and he waved. "Daddy, I'm riding big."

"Yes, you are. You'll be running this show in no time," he teased. They approached him and he lifted Zoe from Maple, a sweet-natured horse—the one he'd outbid Luca on. She was a favorite among guests and good for teaching beginners.

"Can me and Goldie go pway outside?" Zoe asked.

"Not right now." He couldn't risk taking her out. Not today. But he had to burn up her young energy somehow.

"You want to help me feed the horses?" Candy asked. "I have apples for treats today."

Zoe nodded enthusiastically.

"Well, you take Goldie and go wait for me on that bench over there like a big girl and we'll go feed them." Candy motioned her on and Zoe zipped along the arena to the bench near the west entrance and sat, hands folded in her lap, Goldie right beside her.

"Thank you," Nick said. "I need to occupy her for a while. I'm going to be helping with the investigation."

"Garrett and I can keep her, Nick. You know we love her like our own." Candy folded her arms. "We'd never let anything happen to her."

That's what he'd said, too. Less than ten seconds was all it had taken to make a liar of himself.

"And you know I can take care of her seizures." Candy had witnessed them and been trained. He didn't doubt that.

"I know. But I can't put that kind of responsibility on you. It's not fair to you or Garrett. I'm grateful for you, that you love her as if she were your own." Candy had complications that made having a child of her own difficult. They were going through the process to adopt but it was arduous and expensive.

"Okay," she said, her tone laced with disappointment.

"But if you'll let me clear the stable and make sure it's safe, you guys can give the horses their fill of oats and apples for hours. I need to get into the conference room and help Ruby."

"I'm sure she knows how to do her job without being micromanaged," Candy said and walked with him. "I mean, she seems capable. I also noticed your side-glances and lingering looks. Did you feel a spark?" she asked.

Candy. Concerned, observant and nosy. "She's pretty, smart and capable. That's all there is to it. I've known her twenty-four hours tops." He cleared the stable and made sure all entry and exit points were secure, then he kissed Zoe and handed Candy a two-way radio. "Hit me if you need anything."

"We'll be fine."

She had more confidence than he did. He hustled back to the office and found Ruby tacking information to the whiteboard and talking with her team. Freshly brewed coffee clung to the air, along with a faint scent of her flowery perfume. "Zoe and Candy are in the stable."

"Tanner called the landline since there's no cell service—I hope you don't mind me giving them all your number."

"Not at all."

"Jeremy Benedict called in sick the past three days. They went by his house. No vehicle. No Jeremy Benedict. Maybe it's suspicious or maybe he didn't have personal time and said he was sick. It's not uncommon. They'll check back later in the evening." She turned, the marker she was using to write on the whiteboard in hand. "Let's talk about Aaron Millsap. You conducted the investigation and testified at his trial. He maintained his innocence. Did he ever threaten you?"

"No. I mean, the usual. You-got-it-wrong speech, and 'you're making a mistake.' If that can be considered a threat." He shrugged. "I have received other threats, but those inmates haven't gotten out of prison."

"Doesn't mean they haven't set up the situation. I want that list," Ruby said.

They worked for the next three hours, going over scenarios, rivals, everything including everyone from prison who might have a vendetta. They'd gone through two pots of coffee and he'd checked in on Zoe every fifteen minutes until Candy told him to calm down, that things were fine and that Zoe had dozed off with Goldie in a pile of hay. The local cleaning crew had come by to let them know the windows were boarded and the mess cleaned up.

His stomach growled as he heard cars arriving outside. Ruby glanced out the window and grinned. "Jacqueline."

Nick followed her outside to find a fit woman with pretty, dark eyes and equally dark hair that had been coiled in a tight knot on her neck. She smiled, then hugged Ruby. Her German shepherd stood by, watching warily. He was a gorgeous specimen. Black and tan and all muscle.

"I brought you a vehicle. That's what took so long. Waiting on the barge." Jacqueline extended her hand and introduced herself. "Good to meet you. Sorry for the circumstances." She was strong and serious. And former army. He instantly liked her.

"Thank you. I appreciate you coming."

"I'd love to meet Zoe."

"She's napping again at the moment." His radio crackled.

"Eagle eye, the chicken hawk has sprouted her wings," Candy said with a snicker.

"Okay, so Zoe's awake. Come on." He chuckled. "Roger that, turkey," he said into the radio. They followed him into the stable. He loved the smells of hay and leather.

"Turkey, huh?" Candy teased and shook Jacqueline's hand when Ruby introduced her.

Jacqueline beamed at Zoe with sleepy eyes and hay stuck in her dark hair. "I fell asweep, Daddy."

"Naps are good. Be thankful you have time to take them." He picked her up. "This is Jacqueline and this is her dog…"

"Jesse."

"Jesse."

Zoe clung to Nick's neck and did her shy face but spoke. "I wike Jesse. This is my dog, Goldie. She helps me when I get sick sometimes."

Jacqueline smiled. "She's a good doggy. Jesse is, too. But he's a work dog so he doesn't play very much."

"Why don't we go up to the house and have something to eat," Nick offered.

"I want Officer Ruby to carry me, Daddy."

Ruby didn't hesitate and opened her arms. Zoe fell right into them and wrapped her little self around Ruby. "I fed the horsies apples and oats."

"You are so good with them. I could use a snack, too." She hugged Zoe tight, and Nick felt something shift in his chest. He was a little surprised at how quickly Zoe had warmed up to Ruby. She was normally shy. Ruby just had the touch.

Everyone agreed and they headed up to the house,

which had been cleaned up. No glass in sight and the windows had been boarded with plywood.

"Daddy, did the thunder break our windows?" Zoe asked as she saw the wood.

"The big blast sure did." He couldn't lie but he couldn't tell the sobering truth, either. Not to a child. "I have lunch meat for sandwiches, and I make a mean grilled cheese. Is that okay with everyone?"

"I love grilled cheese," Ruby said. "My mom used to make them for me all the time growing up. Until I got old enough, and then it was a staple with cans of tomato soup."

"I may have some of that," Nick said. "Nothing better than grilled cheese and tomato soup."

Jacqueline chuckled. "I'm not a fan of canned soups, but I'm all about a grilled cheese. Can I help you?"

"No, you had a long drive and then a ferry ride. Relax."

"Officer Ruby, can you come pway with me?" Zoe asked and tugged at Ruby's hand.

"I sure can."

"For a few minutes only," Nick said as Zoe tugged Ruby along to her room to play and Jacqueline followed. She'd need Zoe to warm up to her if this was going to work. After he opened the cans of soups and put them on the stove to heat, Ruby returned.

"I'd so rather be in there playing, but we need Zoe to acclimate to Jacqueline. Learn to trust her. It'll make things easier and there'll be less worry over possible seizures. I've filled in Jacqueline on everything, though."

He laid the bread on the counter. "Thank you. Zoe really has taken a quick shine to you."

"The feeling is mutual."

"Gouda or American?" Nick asked.

"Both."

He grinned. "A cheese girl. I like it."

Ruby snickered and snagged a slice of gouda cheese. "I didn't have this fancy cheese growing up. Mom did her best working two jobs. The government helped us out with our cheese."

Nick nodded, appreciating Ruby's candidness about her upbringing. "Both of my parents worked. I never heard them argue about money until after Lizzie went missing. Then the bills mounted up. They ran up credit cards to pay private investigators and companies to search for her. But nothing. That's part of why I wanted to go into law enforcement. I suppose in my kid brain I thought I'd actually be able to locate her and she'd come home safe and sound."

But that hadn't happened and when he went into the army as military police, then CID, he realized that those men likely exhausted themselves searching. Some cases simply went cold at no fault of the investigators. But Mom kept insisting and Dad kept honoring her wishes. They'd ended up filing for bankruptcy when he was thirteen. They'd stayed in the area but moved homes and neighborhoods. Nothing was the same.

"I'm sorry. I know that must have been hard on all of you."

"I feel like I raised myself in some respects." He shrugged and buttered bread for the sandwiches.

"Me, too. My dad was in the area but never in the picture. I felt to blame."

"I get that." He laid the buttered bread on the griddle, and it sizzled, then he stirred the soup.

The landline rung and Nick answered, then handed Ruby the phone. "It's Officer Ford."

"Hey, Tanner, what's up?" She listened for a moment, then her mouth dropped open.

"What is it?" Nick asked.

She glanced up. "They found Jeremy Benedict."

"Where is he?"

"The woods near your house. He's dead. Blunt-force trauma."

SIX

Ruby pinched the bridge of her nose. One of their persons of interest was dead. Britta had alerted Tanner, which is how they'd found Jeremy Benedict. That meant it was possible that Jeremy was their shooter and abductor... or the scent of the real killer/abductor/shooter had been transferred to him in a scuffle and he was an innocent bystander. Tanner and Parker were going to ask around about Jeremy and they couldn't ignore that they'd found a rifle on his person. They'd see if it was a match to the bullets found in the house.

They also found a receipt from the Harlequin Campground nearby. If Jeremy lived in the area, then why was he at the Harlequin Campground only two days prior? And if he'd called in sick, why was he at a campsite? Ruby needed answers and was going to get some today.

Jeremy looked good for the crimes. But Ruby wasn't relying on appearances or surface information. Eli had presented himself as charming and charismatic. He'd been generous in his gifts and given her undivided attention, when her own work hadn't been calling. And yet, it appeared he might be far more than a handsome suitor.

He might be a killer.

That was too much to handle. So she shoved it down

deep, along with her other hurts, insecurities and second guesses.

Nick stood by the plates of untouched grilled cheese sandwiches and the pot of soup but kept silent. She liked that he'd picked up on the fact that she was internally processing. Zoe came running with a squeal, and Jacqueline followed along with Goldie. Pepper perked up, realized all was well and resumed her position, casually lying at Ruby's feet.

Jacqueline paused. "What's going on?"

"I'll fill you in later," she said and nodded with her chin toward Zoe.

"Okay. Well, Zoe and I couldn't finish the tea party without Officer Ruby so we put a pin in it. We've been building a pink-and-purple palace with her oversize building blocks. I gotta say, she's quite the architect." She accepted a grilled cheese from Nick and joined Zoe at the kitchen table.

"We got boards for windows. That's siwwy," Zoe said and climbed into Ruby's lap with her plate. Ruby didn't mind at all. In fact, she loved it. Like her lap had been made just for it. It was hard not becoming attached. Zoe Rossi was easy to attach to.

Zoe bit into her sandwich, a string of cheese hanging from her little chin.

"That is silly," Ruby said and handed her a napkin and took a spoonful of soup.

Nick opened a bag of plain potato chips and they all made small talk while eating since Zoe was with them. After Zoe was done, she asked to watch her favorite movie with the fish who forgets her name. Nick got it all set up and returned to the table.

"How are you and Zoe warming up?"

Jacqueline smiled. "Pretty good."

"Jacqueline is great with kids," Ruby said. "But don't let her soft side fool you. She can also lay you out in five seconds flat if necessary."

Jacqueline laughed.

"I've seen it. Chasing a thief in Mount Rainier. String of thefts. He was almost three times her size. New on the job. I instantly loved her." She reached into the bag of chips and snagged a few, laying them on her plate.

"That makes me feel better leaving Zoe in your hands. I think we need to move fast. It's getting worse as time goes by. Jeremy a casualty?"

"Or he was behind it," Ruby said.

"Then who shot him?"

"A woman led Zoe away. Not a man. And then there's the woman who distracted you by dropping her purse, though we're not sure if she set you up or if the other woman just used it as an opportunity. But that means three people might be involved. Could Jeremy—who left your employment and was known to bad-mouth you— have somehow teamed up with Aaron Millsap, the guy you put away? Aaron had a girlfriend. Maybe Jeremy did, too. We can't rule it out."

Nick scooted his plate away and rubbed the back of his neck. "I know. All of it is plausible."

"Don't worry about Zoe," Jacqueline said. "You guys need to get out there and find this person or people. We'll be good here and you can call and check in all you like."

Nick nodded and went to tell Zoe he was leaving for just a little bit with Officer Ruby.

"She's a sweet kiddo. I see you've become more than protective-duty fond of her," Jacqueline said.

"My maternal heartstrings are keyed up." She grinned.

Zoe jumped up and ran for Ruby. "Officer Ruby, I will miss you."

"I'll miss you, too, punkin. You and Officer Jacqueline have fun with Goldie and Jesse."

"We will. And Pepper."

"Pepper has to go with Officer Ruby, like Goldie goes everywhere with you," Nick said.

"Oh. Does she get the shivers, too?" Zoe looked at Ruby, melting her heart. She must call seizures "shivers."

"No. But Pepper helps Ruby work. She finds lost people in the park."

Zoe nodded. "Is someone wost in the park now?"

"Sort of." He kissed her forehead then traded contact information with Jacqueline, gave her the rundown of Zoe's routine, showed her where the medicine cabinet was, then handed her a printed-out treatment plan and a list of numbers if anything happened, plus a set of keys to his Ford truck if they needed to leave, or what he didn't say—flee. After fifteen minutes, they walked outside to Ruby's silver PNK9 SUV that Jacqueline had brought over on the barge. Ruby opened the back driver's-side door, and Pepper hopped inside.

Nick slid into the passenger seat, then cast a glance back toward the house. She could tell him not to worry all day long and remind him of Jacqueline's competency, but that was his prized treasure inside and nothing would keep him from being concerned. She silently prayed that he would have peace and God would protect Zoe and Jacqueline, and that they'd find this person or people ASAP.

Ruby poured some water she'd brought into the dog bowl that was secured in the back seat. Pepper waited patiently then went for a nice long drink as Ruby closed the door and took her seat in the driver's side. She rolled the back windows down. The mesh that covered the windows kept Pepper safe from jumping out—not that she would— but also prevented someone from smashing a window to get to her. And it gave her fresh air, which she loved.

"Where to first?" Nick asked.

"Let's go to Harlequin Campground. See if we can talk to anyone who might have seen Jeremy Benedict."

She plugged the address into her navigation system and headed north on Stehekin Valley Road toward Imus Trail. Flanked by gorgeous mountains and evergreens, Ruby was glad she'd moved to the Pacific Northwest, even if she'd been running away from Alabama, from personal pain and hurt.

The narrow road wound through the mountains and was empty, but behind them a car swooped around the bend. No big deal, but the hairs on Ruby's arms stood at attention and she gripped the wheel.

"What's wrong?" Nick asked.

"Nothing." She glanced in her side mirror at the dark truck, navy blue or maybe black. Tinted windows. "I guess I'm jumpy."

Nick leaned toward his window and looked into the side mirror as they passed the post office. "It's gaining on us."

No sooner than he had gotten the words out of his mouth than the truck rammed into the back of the SUV and Pepper barked. "Hold on, girl." Ruby gripped the wheel tighter and pressed down on the gas as they took a sharp turn, but the truck accelerated, too.

They were almost to Purple Point Campground which was before Harlequin Campground and the lake was to their right. Ruby refrained from shrieking as the truck rammed into them again and she cut a hard left, her foot still heavy on the gas as they raced into the wooded area.

Nick leaned over and grabbed the wheel, steering right just in time to dodge a large tree. Ruby slammed on the brakes.

Pepper whimpered and Ruby opened the door from the back seat into the front. The dog leaped into the middle and nuzzled Ruby's neck. Ruby let out a heavy breath and looked at Nick. His eyes were filled with a slow-burning fury.

"Thank you," she said breathlessly. If he hadn't reached over and grabbed the wheel, they'd have hit that solid trunk head on and ended up unconscious.

The driver of the truck had done their job, she supposed, and had already sped away. "I think they were hoping to push us into the lake."

Nick huffed. "Turning left was a smart move."

Except instead of letting off the gas pedal, she'd kept her foot's weight on it and nearly killed them. She balled her hands to keep them from trembling as the SUV quietly idled. She said a silent prayer of thanks to God for keeping them safe.

"Let's get to the campground. I can't run underground like a scared rabbit. I have a job to do. A killer to catch. But you don't have to be a part of this, Nick. I can't help but go into dangerous situations. I don't have the luxury. You? You could get Zoe and get out of town. Lay low somewhere for a while."

"And hope we're no longer a target? Hope that someone will find this person? I still have a business to run. The bills aren't going to excuse me or give me a pass because I'm in a serious situation. I can't even be sure we wouldn't be followed. I had no idea we were being watched, but we must be, or how would that truck have known where we were?"

That was a good question. "Maybe we're not being watched. Maybe someone close to you is leaking your whereabouts to the bad guy."

Nick's heart was almost beating out of his chest, but his head was cool and composed. Instead of feeling afraid, he was channeling that fear into focus. Whoever was doing this was going down. End of story. He reached over and laid his hand over Ruby's. She was holding up well, but he could sense how rattled she was. It was normal. He was rattled, too. The thought of someone in his closest circle in cahoots with someone was mind-boggling.

"You okay to drive or do we need to take a break?" he asked.

"No." She put the vehicle in Reverse. "No breaks. But do think about what I said."

"I am. I just can't imagine anyone on my team leaking information and putting me or my daughter in harm's way. They all love Zoe. And I've never had a real argument with any of them or had to give them a corrective plan of action. I pay well and I'm fair. So... I just don't know."

"Well, Dylan and Brandie will be talking to them and should be able to shed some insightful light."

"No one even knew where we were going but Candy."

"I know it's hard to believe someone you think is a good, kind person could be deceptive or have a secret life, but it's possible." Ruby pulled onto the road and it sounded like something was being dragged. She pulled over, and Nick hopped out and yanked away a wiry limb that had been caught underneath the car. When he got back inside, she was massaging her temples.

"Sounds to me like you had a bad experience with someone you trusted." And she might be projecting. But he'd refrain from spewing that.

"I did. Fairly recently. I dated a guy who was a prominent businessman. He was kind and romantic. Generous. But he might be linked to a murder case we're working. I can't say much more, as it's confidential."

"I understand. And it's not like you're using names or anything." But he had read about a lodge owner and her boyfriend being gunned down in Mount Rainier National Park several months ago and that the suspect was a member of the PNK9 team. He'd kept himself from telling her that he had opposed a PNK9 officer initially coming to search for Zoe due to what he'd read online. Now he was glad his protests landed on deaf ears. Ruby had been top-notch and professional. One bad apple could spoil the whole basket, but that wasn't necessarily the case each time.

"Yeah, but unless you live under a rock you know there's some stuff going on with the PNK9 unit."

"I have read about it online. I'm sorry."

"Me, too. And as far as Mara Gilmore, I don't think she could kill someone in cold blood. Even though the circumstantial evidence says otherwise. But then…we have other leads that might prove she's being framed." She gripped the wheel again and he wondered if the man she thought was a good guy might be involved with a possible framing. That would stink on so many levels.

"Why don't we call it and come back in the morning. I'd like to get home to Zoe."

Ruby agreed and they headed back to his house in silence.

A killer was out there and willing to do anything to get to Zoe.

* * *

Nick and Ruby left early the next day to head back to the Harlequin Campground. No Labor Day rest for them today. They approached the Stehekin Pastry Company. "You ever been to Stehekin before now?" he asked.

"No, actually." Like a little secret in North Cascades Park. Away from the hustle and bustle.

"Pull over. I know we have work to do, but I feel like we deserve to treat ourselves after that fiasco yesterday and I can't turn down a sticky bun."

Ruby pulled into a small parking area. The air outside the rustic cabin was permeated with the scents of vanilla, cinnamon and an all-around good time. A few bikes were placed in bike racks and patrons sat at picnic tables enjoying their sweets.

Inside, they ordered two sticky buns and two cups of coffee and then made their way out with their purchases and sat a picnic table under a tree that was a little more secluded. They had a good eye of the street, where they could watch for a dark-colored truck.

Pepper sat beside Ruby, and she rubbed her head, then gave her a dog treat to enjoy before whipping out her lint roller and rolling it down her pant legs. She adored dogs. The hair on her pants—or her coworkers pants—not so much. "I don't give her table food other than frozen blueberries and occasionally scrambled eggs. But I do keep treats and dog cookies on hand."

"Have you always loved dogs?"

"I had a yellow Lab growing up. My mom got him from the pound, and he was my best friend. I told him all my secrets and his fur held a lot of tears. But don't think my childhood was depressing. I have far more better memories than sad ones. Church camp in the summer and fish frys at the end of summer with my mom's side of the family. When Yeller passed, I knew I could never be without a dog. So joining a K-9 unit made sense to me."

They ate in silence for a few moments.

"This is good," Ruby said. "I've been thinking about our suspects," she added, glancing at him. "I know you don't want to believe the worst in a coworker—you know I get it—but you have to talk to me about your employees. All of them."

"Fine, but can I at least enjoy the sticky bun before all the talk leaves a sour taste in my mouth."

"Fair enough. Did you have a pet growing up?"

"No. My parents were too busy to take care of pets, and my dad had bad allergies. I remember our babysitter, Hailey, had a long-haired cat, and when she'd come over, he would go into sneezing fits and sneeze for a day after she left, but we loved her so Dad endured. Dander was not his friend."

"My babysitter had a dog. A beagle named Snoopy. She used to bring her over all the time. I have no idea what happened to her. Once I turned ten, my mom let me stay home alone. She was usually home by seven most nights and on late nights, I stayed with my grandmama."

Nick sipped his coffee. "After Lizzie went missing, my parents didn't want to leave me. They got overprotective and so Hailey never babysat me again. I hated that because she was so much fun. She really loved us. Now, I think would I let a fifteen-year-old babysit Zoe? That's pretty young." He laughed. "Back then I thought she was large and in charge. Fifteen. I guess it is standard babysitter age, though." He shook his head and Ruby grinned.

"I imagine that was tough, too. Losing another person you loved, in a way."

"It was." He finished off the caramelized sticky bun and picked the few leftover nuts on the paper wrapper, then licked his fingers. "That hit the spot."

"It did." Though, Ruby hadn't finished hers yet.

He waited and chatted while she finished every bite then they tossed their trash and took their to-go coffee cups with them. Ruby paused. "I see the pastry company owners also rent cabins. Saw the brochures inside."

"Three. Well, four now I believe. One is pretty remote, though. Why?"

"If Aaron Millsap is our guy and he's here in Stehekin, he has to either be camping or in a cabin. Let's find out before we move on to Harlequin Campground."

"Good idea," Nick said.

"You said one of the cabins is remote—let's check that one out first."

They went back inside and talked with the owners. No one had rented the remote cabin in the past couple of weeks. It was vacant. Vacant could mean squatters. After getting a list of names of guests in the cabins in the past month, they got back inside the SUV and Ruby started the engine while they perused the names on the list.

"Any name ring a bell?" she asked, pulling out of the spot and heading in the direction of the remote cabin.

"No. We can use this to match up the ones I arrested. Too many for me to remember them all. Sadly." Nick had been weighed down by the all the cruelty and violence people enacted, especially on women and children during his CID days.

He'd prayed and asked God to give him peace. Some days it seemed He did. Then another crime would happen or a TV show would be on and Lizzie's abduction would come flooding back. How did one get peace and then hang on to it for the duration? It seemed like catching lightning bugs. You'd get one and see the light shine from inside your closed palm, only to open your hand to see it up close then lose it to the night air.

"The cabin is six and a half miles down the Stehekin River." They found the access road and Ruby grunted. "I don't think a vehicle is going to get us there. We need a UTV. But I don't want to bring the owners into this. If someone is squatting…we know they're armed."

Nick agreed. "Well, you up for a six-and-a-half-mile hike?"

"I did inhale that entire sticky bun."

Nick laughed. Ruby could handle a full sticky bun. She parked on the side of a narrow dirt road. He opened his door and stepped out, pulling his weapon just in case. Ruby did the same and Pepper bounded out beside her.

"Okay. Let's do this."

They began the trek. A light breeze rustled the trees as they hiked the rugged and remote terrain uphill toward the cabin. Even during daylight, the atmosphere that should be refreshing as fall approached felt ominous.

Nick checked his step counter. One mile ticked by, two…three…

At about five miles, Ruby spoke up. "You thought any more on who could be working on the inside?"

"A Judas among my inner circle?" Nick asked. "No. No, I can't. But I have been thinking about this situation for lack of a better term. Nightmare seems to fit."

"That it does. Once we get back, we'll talk with Dylan and Brandie. Get their thoughts. I need to contact everyone to meet up after dinner and debrief. Or maybe we'll just wait until tomorrow morning. It's going to be a long day for everyone. We'll all need a good night's sleep after a full day of working. Exhaustion and burning the midnight oil does no one any good. Though I know you want to go full force until this person or people are found. I feel that."

"I also know that I'm one man and not a machine. I need food and rest and sleep. I would like to check in on Zoe and Jacqueline. I'm sure no news is good news."

"I'm sure it is. But feel free. I'm watching."

Nick reached into his pocket to retrieve his phone just as the crack sounded and a bullet landed in front of his feet, spraying dirt into the air.

"Take cover!" Nick hollered and dove on top of Ruby.

SEVEN

Another bullet slammed into the earth beside Nick and Ruby. Nick held her tight as they rolled together down the hill toward the pond and away from the bullets.

Somewhere in the trees, the shooter had found them. Again.

They rolled like rocks until they hit the bottom of the hill, then Nick braced them to keep them from landing in the water.

Pepper had run with them and was alert and attentive to her handler. "Good girl," Ruby said, debris lodged in her hair. The cabin was half a mile up. Nick didn't think the shooter was professional or they'd have been dead—at least he would have been. But the perp was still a good shot. He wasn't sure if the better option was to run toward the cabin or try to get around the pond while they had the hill to safeguard them.

"Let's stay along the edge of the hill and move toward the cabin. We can secure and take a united front on whoever approaches," Ruby said.

"They won't approach if they have a scope. We're not safe anywhere." His heart beat furiously within his chest, and sweat broke out along his temples. "But I agree it's more solid of a cover. Let's go before he makes his way to the hill. Then we are doomed."

They ran in a crouched position along the bottom of the hill, keeping an eye at the crest and knowing they'd have to trek up it to the cabin, putting them out in the open. The area was remote. There were too many places to hide. And if more than one person was in this together, one might be shooting and others could be inside the cabin.

They were in a bad state of affairs.

Nick took the lead on the ascent, praying they'd be protected. "Once we get to the opening, we have to book it to the cabin. It's going to be a little bit of a haul. But it's where we are, Ruby."

"Agreed."

Nick grabbed her hand and squeezed then led the charge up to the hill. As he reached the top, he froze.

Ruby slammed into his back then gasped.

Pepper growled and Ruby quietly hushed her.

Ten feet away were a mama black bear and three cubs.

"Don't…move…" Ruby whispered. "Make yourself look as big as possible and look directly at her."

The threat level just escalated by a billion percent. His Glock wasn't going to do much to a bear and he didn't want to hurt her. She had babies to care for and her reaction would be normal. But they couldn't run for cover because running would set her off. So they had to stand like frozen targets, but a shooter was out there and standing still would get them killed, too.

Ruby's hand rested on his shoulder. "Has she seen us?"

As she asked, the mama bear raised her head. Nick was certain she'd known but now she was curious. She chomped her teeth and pawed the dirt, then snarled, warning them they were too close to her and her babies.

"I'm gonna go with yes," he whispered. "Our only choice is back down the hill, but if she comes, we really have nowhere to go, and I don't want to shoot her." That would likely make her madder than kill her, anyway.

"Hold your ground. I learned this from my friend Everly. She's a bear expert."

"Well, I wish she was here now."

"Same. The cabin is our best shot."

"Yep." Nick put his hands out and slowly inched sideways. The bear snarled and pawed again, this time with more aggression. "Just keep going. No sudden movements."

"I have bear spray. It'll sting but it won't hurt her. It's in my right hand." Her left still rested on his left shoulder as they moved in side-step together toward the cabin, hoping and praying they made it without danger. "Why aren't we being shot at?" Ruby asked. "Not that I'm complaining."

Mama Bear moved toward them, but the cubs had gone into the woods.

"Maybe the shooter is waiting to see if a bear will take us out and do the dirty work for him."

"How kind of him."

The house was ten feet away, but even if they made it, the doors would be locked.

Another snap of the jaws and more pronounced swatting of the ground, and Mama Bear was done playing.

Gunfire cracked the sky and Nick flinched, but the bullet landed two feet in front of the bear, spraying dirt and angering her further. Mission accomplished.

The bear began to charge. Nick and Ruby and Pepper raced toward the cabin, but the bear was fast. Too fast.

Gaining.

But the bullets ceased. The shooter must be watching from an unknown location. No time to think about that now.

So much for not running.

They reached the porch as the black bear made it to the edge of the house. Nick turned the knob.

The bear barreled onto the porch. Pepper growled and her hackles raised.

Ruby sprayed the bear spray in the bright orange cylinder long enough for Nick to open the unlocked door. They bolted inside and locked it, but if that bear wanted in, she was getting inside. As they entered the living room, a bullet slammed into the front living-room window, shattering glass all around.

Nick grabbed Ruby's hand and pulled her down. They had no cell signal. Nothing. It was just them, the bear and the shooter.

"Upstairs." Safer from the bear and the shooter. No stairs, but there was a ladder leading up. They climbed it to a bedroom and one bathroom. Nick peeked outside the window. The shooter was hidden in the trees, but there was no sound from the bear. "Well, the upside is… no one is home, Goldilocks."

"That all depends on how literal you're being in this story. I think Mama Bear wants us gone."

The teasing lightened the tension and fear coursing through their veins. "We can't leave. The bear is out there. Haven't given her enough time to get a safe enough distance away. And yet the shooter might be making his way to us as we speak."

"You really look at things with the glass half full, don't you?" Ruby asked, her breath shaky.

"Ruby, we don't even have a glass right now." He peeped over the ladder to the ground floor. No more shots. No sound of any movement in the house. "I'm going to check it out. Weigh our options. You stay here."

"I don't think so."

He turned and saw the resolute expression on her face. "Fine. We'll both go. Just watch your back…and mine."

"Same." They eased back down the ladder, waiting a few beats at each rung to listen and hope for the best. Finally, they reached the first floor.

No active sound.

The only way to test their safety was to step out and be bait. If the shooter was watching through a scope, he'd see them. And he'd shoot.

"Doesn't look like anyone has been squatting. Beds are made with no imprints. At least upstairs. Nothing in this kitchen that tells me it's been used." Ruby squatted low and moved toward the downstairs bedroom. A few seconds later, she softly called, "Clear."

So it was an empty cabin.

"Wait," she said. "I found something."

"What?"

She returned with something in her hand. "Maybe it's nothing but this place is swept clean, minus all the glass. I'd find it hard to believe the cleaning people left this or didn't see it. It was lying beside the trash can, which had a fresh liner in it."

He glanced at what Ruby held.

An empty pack of Camel unfiltered cigarettes.

Nick's stomach dropped as his thoughts went back to the past, when he arrested Aaron Millsap for attempted kidnapping. He'd had a pack of the same brand in his front shirt pocket and one hanging from his lip. The smoke had curled and burned Nick's eyes.

"Aaron Millsap is in Stehekin," he said.

And he was here for revenge.

Ruby had her kit with her in the backpack she had on. She opened it and put on a pair of latex gloves, then bagged the cigarette box. "Nick, you and I both know an empty pack of cigarettes doesn't confirm that Aaron Millsap is in Stehekin or responsible for Zoe's abduction or the attempted murders. This could be anyone's. But I agree—it's probable." She put the evidence bag in her backpack. "If it is his, he meant to toss it in the trash and missed, although why? Why would he do that? Wouldn't he want to keep his squatting here hidden?"

"Maybe he was coming back. Got a little busy shooting us in the woods. It explains how he spotted us. If he'd come back here and seen us, he had time to get into the woods and take position."

Ruby frowned. "Where's the truck he tried to run us off the road then?" Nick had some really good points, but he was also emotionally invested and wasn't seeing objectively or clearly, and that was another reason she'd hesitated to bring him into the investigation. She needed unbiased work.

"He could have it stashed in the woods or something. This area is so remote no one would know. And before you ask how would he even know about these cabins, anyone can go online and google Stehekin, watch YouTube videos and discover the place. It's not a big place."

Okay, maybe he was thinking more clearly than Ruby originally thought.

"He would know he'd have to bring his truck in on a ferry. We need to look at the manifesto and see if a blue Ford truck was sent over in the past month. I wouldn't think he'd be here any longer. Maybe only a week. He can't squat here forever. He could have even inquired about the cabin to see when it would be booked. Or they might have an online booking, which would show when dates were open and blocked off. It wouldn't be that difficult."

Now he was making excellent sense. It was possible he laid the pack on the nightstand and it simply fell off beside the trash can. He might have planned on coming back, staying, covering his tracks. But they'd shown up. If the cigarettes belonged to Aaron Millsap, then the chances of prints on the pack were decent.

And maybe they'd have a solid lead and could put a good foot forward instead of reacting all the time and running. Right now, the jerk with the gun and the truck had the upper hand. Ruby was ready to turn the tables.

The area had grown quiet. Either the shooter had given up and gotten spooked by a very angry bear who'd been blasted with bear spray, or he was still lying in wait. If it was Aaron Millsap, he'd learned patience in prison. Plotting, planning and preparing for the great revengeful escapade. He could sit in the forest for hours. He'd had nowhere to be, or go to, in prison. Waiting was not going to be a problem for him.

"I'm going to see if the bear is gone," Ruby whispered and left the bedroom, but she heard Nick's quiet footfalls behind her. When she reached the living and kitchen area, she paused. The two front windows had been blown out. Glass littered the floor. A few pieces had reached the kitchen. She slowly moved, crouching into the living area, her breath caught in her lungs.

So far, so good.

She moved into the kitchen and to the back door they'd run through when the bear had attacked. Back to the wall, she side-glanced through the kitchen door panes. Looked clear. No animals on the back porch. Slowly, she inched the door open, gun in hand, and got a better look at her surroundings.

She motioned Nick to follow and she stepped outside. Gun in her right hand, bear spray in her left…just in case. Somewhere out there was a surly fur mama, and they had a six-and-half-mile hike back down.

"I think I should contact Dylan and Brandie. Have them come on a UTV. Park rangers will allow use of one. We work with them all the time. I don't like the distance we'll be in the open. The shooter might be counting on it and waiting for us to get closer to our vehicle."

"Agreed."

She used her satellite phone and called Dylan. She gave him the rundown.

"Maced a bear, huh?"

"I wouldn't describe it exactly like that and our lives were at stake."

Dylan chuckled. "You don't have to apologize to me. Better than shooting it, and in the end, she'll be fine. I mean, she might be more likely to be waiting for you in the woods than the shooter."

Ruby rolled her eyes but grinned. "So will you come get us?"

"If you put the bear spray up." He laughed again. "We're actually a few minutes from the ranger station. We talked with Nick's employees."

"And?" Ruby asked.

"They all sang his praises. He pays well, is kind and fair. Works hard, expects them to as well. Knows the terrain. Loves his kid. But Priscilla Overton, the main trail guide for families, she's good friends with Yolanda Martin, who Nick fired for keying his car. When I asked her about that, she said all the right things, but her body language betrayed her. When I called her out, she admitted that Yolanda shouldn't have been fired and Nick had given Yolanda mixed signals—it wasn't her fault for misreading them, granted she should have had to pay for the damages but not lost her job. She followed it up with the fact that Nick was a great guy and probably didn't realize he was giving her mixed signals."

Interesting. Zoe would have known Yolanda and Priscilla, but not if disguised. And it didn't explain the mysterious woman who might have purposely spilled the contents of her purse as a ruse to get Nick's attention off Zoe for a few seconds. Of course, Priscilla and Yolanda could have friends.

"Can you have Jasmin see if there's any connection between Priscilla and Yolanda, and Aaron Millsap? It's a long shot, but I'm willing to make stretches." According to the guy Nick had talked to, Aaron had a girlfriend. But they weren't sure who it was. What if it was Priscilla or Yolanda? Better to check it than end up wrong and dead.

"I'll get her on it. You sit tight. We'll be there in about twenty, thirty minutes."

With Dylan and his wild driving and love for all things fast, she guessed it would be more like fifteen minutes. "Thanks."

She turned to Nick. "I guess you got the gist of that."

He nodded. "I wasn't giving her mixed signals. Honest."

"I believe you. She's young. Infatuated. She wanted any nicety to be more, mean more." Sadly, Ruby could relate. That first day she'd met Eli, he'd complimented her way with Pepper and she'd instantly thought it was flirting. Then she'd heard him compliment her colleague Willow, too. That should have been a sign, but maybe she was that starved for male love and affection.

Instead, she'd subtly flirted with him and he must have caught on. Then it became a little back-and-forth until he asked her to dinner at the lodge. She'd accepted. Of course, he wasn't a suspect when she'd began dating him. He had an alibi for Stacey Stark and Jonas Digby's murders. And, yeah, a K-9 alerted that he'd had guns in the basement of one of the lodges he and Stacy ran together, but he'd been open about it and had had a good explanation for storing family hunting rifles down there.

But there had been no way to discount the new information that made Eli Ballard look guilty of the murders... and of a cover-up. Mara had texted her brother, Asher, that both his life and their father's had been threatened and *that* was why she had to stay in hiding and was afraid to reveal what she might know. And then evidence—a photo had surfaced of Mara and Asher's father, who had dementia, at the assisted-living center where he lived... and Eli had been seen there. Eli had no connection to the Gilmores otherwise. So why had been there?

He might have snowed them all.

"What are you thinking?" Nick asked. "I know it's not our case. I can tell by the shift in your facial expression." He pointed to her fists. "And it's upsetting you. You want to talk? We have thirty minutes."

She grinned. "No, we don't. Not if Dylan's driving." But the fact that he could read her and was delicate with her warmed her heart. And told her there was no way he gave Yolanda Martin mixed signals. He was nothing like Eli Ballard. "You were a good investigator. I can tell."

"I'd like to think so. I enjoyed the job—not the depravity but the justice."

"You could always go back to it. You're not old. Keep your outfitter and work as a park agent."

Nick's sideways grin tilted her heart. "You're redirecting. So I'll take that as a no. You don't want to talk about what you're thinking."

Adept. "See. You might be letting your real calling slip away."

His eyes flashed with disappointment. "Sad that my calling came from tragedy."

"I think callings often do. My grandmama used to tell me the best ministry was when one made their mess their ministry. You can reach people others can't because you walked or were dragged down the same bumpy road."

"Sounds like you have a wise grandmama."

"I did. I miss her. If she hadn't passed, I might not have left Alabama."

Nick held her gaze for a beat, then two. "I'm sorry for your loss. But I'm glad you did leave and that you're here. I am sorry we met under these circumstances."

She was not going to jump on that like a dog with a bone and assume it meant something personal. He was talking professionally. "I appreciate that."

The sound of a UTV broke the moment and then Dylan came into view. His big Saint Bernard, Ridge, was in the passenger seat, wearing his hilarious goggles.

Dylan approached with a grin on his face. "Someone call for a ride?"

Ruby laughed and shook her head, then laughed at

Ridge's black doggy shirt with white lettering. I Can't Help But Get My Dander Up.

Now to make it the miles back to the SUV without another incident.

EIGHT

Tuesday morning came with the perfect trail riding weather. The stables were full of tourists signing up and wanting to take horses to Rainbow Falls and have picnics. Business was good. Nick listened to the coffeepot in the conference room drip and fill the place with rich roasted caffeine. Candy had come in early, before 8:00 a.m., to get set up for the day and brought a box of sticky buns and cinnamon rolls from the Stehekin Pastry Company. They were sitting on the small table by the coffeepot.

Ruby had called a meeting for 9:00 a.m., giving everyone time for extra rest. Dylan and Brandie had seen to getting the cigarette pack to the lab for analysis. Nick had made the call to the pastry company owners and broken the news about the windows and the possibility of a killer squatting in the cabin. They took it with grace. It didn't hurt that Nick offered to pay for the damages and cleanup. It was the very least he could do.

And if he wasn't already enjoying Ruby's company more than he should have, seeing her and Zoe play *Candy Land* while the dogs watched curiously last night after their long work day was sealing the deal. They'd colored, played with Play-Doh, which he was never going to get out of her bedroom carpet floor, read books and watched a movie about a cartoon fish. Zoe loved that movie. He'd had to put a small fish tank in her room with clown fish. Goldie really loved watching them. If only the days could be full of *Candy Land* and coloring. Zoe had really connected with Ruby, but she also liked Jacqueline, and while he and Ruby were working, she'd played and had fun with her. More importantly, Jacqueline had the skills to safeguard her when he and Ruby couldn't.

Zoe was staying on routine, feeling comfortable and not seizing. He praised the Lord for that. The cabin door opened, and he went on alert, then heard Ruby.

"Nick, it's me." She entered the room in her PNK9 uniform. She looked good in green. Ruby likely looked good in anything. He hadn't been attracted to anyone since Penelope. He didn't feel guilty so much as sad. But there was a new ember, one that had quickly been stoked.

"Good morning. Thanks for the forewarning it was you."

"Maybe keep the door locked." She grinned, fresh-faced and jovial. Even after all that had happened yesterday, she was upbeat. And he loved that Southern accent. It only added to her charm and appeal.

"Maybe I should." But the thought of locking her out unsettled him. He couldn't be falling for a woman he'd only known a few days. That would be weird. Right? Must be all the danger happening. The fact that she'd rescued his daughter and clearly cared for her. He poured her a cup of coffee, added cream, as she liked, and handed her the small foam cup. "You sleep well?"

"I did. How about you?"

"Not really. But then I never sleep deep. Not since Zoe was born." Having children made a person keep at least one eye and ear open. And deep sleeps were no more. "How long do you think it'll take to get the print results from the lab?"

She blew out a breath and retrieved the lint roller she kept on her belt like a gun and rubbed it on her legs, giving Pepper a scolding, but loving, look. "I should have named you Shedder." She ripped the piece of tape covered in black fur and tossed it, then gave him her attention. "Dylan put a rush on it. We'll see. A day or two maybe. Can't say. You know this."

"I'm antsy."

"Maybe make decaf." She raised an eyebrow and tossed him a sly grin. "For yourself, anyway."

"Ha. Ha." If the circumstances hadn't been dire, he'd have asked her to a nice dinner. They could get to know one another better. He might even be tempted to kiss her. He cleared his throat and the thought shook away... like it ought to. "You always been an early riser?" She'd pushed the meeting back, but she was here forty-five minutes early.

"My mom left for work before six every morning and I liked to hug her goodbye because I knew I wouldn't see her again until almost eight at night. Maybe later if she worked late at her second job. As a kid you know they're gone for a long time, but you don't realize until you're grown, working and paying bills and feeling it in your feet and back that all those long hours gone were legit grueling and tiring. No wonder on Sundays after church she slept like the dead. I would hate that she wouldn't take me places on Sunday afternoons, even for ice cream. Now I know she'd had every ounce of energy zapped. I know she wanted to. Wished to. But Monday would roll around, and she'd do it all again. Factory work and waitressing. Neither were sit-down jobs or easy. My mama is my hero. I'm glad she's happy, in a good place financially and with someone who loves her. So I say all that to say some habits die hard."

"She sounds amazing. Hard-working and determined. I think she passed it on." He held her gaze until she lowered her sight to the floor, her long lashes fanning out along her skin.

"Thank you," she said shyly, then looked back at him. "If we're handing out compliments, I admire the way you are with Zoe. Not every dad would be so involved, would protect and love their daughter like you do. That's heartwarming to see." She'd mentioned her dad was in the area, but not the picture. He couldn't imagine knowing Zoe was nearby and not being a part of her life, not seeing her grow up, seeing her accomplishments, hearing her laugh. Knowing her.

"Thank you. I'm sorry you didn't see much of your dad."

"I saw him at the grocery store more than I saw him at my house. Or his. It was so hard seeing my friends who had dads in their lives. I wanted that so badly. Could get so jealous. I stopped asking my mom about him when I was sixteen. I finally saw the pain in her eyes. The regret. The loss. His empty promises."

Nick took her hand but said nothing. Sometimes there were no words for pain. Just contact. Nearness. Two open ears and one closed mouth.

"She didn't date ever again. Not until I graduated from college and had a job with the PD. Then she met Ray and her eyes were brighter than I'd ever seen. I wanted that for her. Ray's a welder and sells cars on the side. He told her to quit both jobs if she wanted to and if she really wanted to work it was her choice. So she helps him with the cars. Sometimes it takes a lifetime to find a Ray."

"You're right. And then sometimes the Ray disappears." She squeezed his hand.

"But there are other Rays out there. Right?"

Her smile was forlorn. "I hope so. I haven't found the first one yet. Thought I did. Twice. But I've been burned more than I've been embraced." She shrugged. "I clearly have crummy judgment."

Nick cocked his head. "I don't know. You seem to want to see the best in others. Maybe you did see the best in those others. You just didn't see the worst. And the worst was bigger than the best. You'll find him."

"Maybe." She sighed and grabbed a sticky bun. "Right now I want to find one perp, or a group of them. I want to make sure you and Zoe are safe and I want this sticky bun. I may have to hike another six and a half miles, but it will be worth every step."

"Agreed."

They ate sticky buns, drank more coffee and kept the conversation light. She shared about her job with the Mobile PD, her love for fresh gulf shrimp, crab and pretty much all things seafood. Her dreams to own a whole kennel of rescue dogs, her shock that he'd never had shrimp and grits or just grits ever in his life. She promised to make it for him because no one should be without that experience. He laughed a lot. More than he had in a long time, and it surprised him he could with everything going on. But he needed it and thanked God for it.

He told her about how he fell out of a tree fort and broke his arm in two places. Their babysitter, Hailey, had driven him to the hospital in his mom's car on only her permit and she could barely see over the steering wheel. He'd been more afraid of a car crash than the pain in his arm.

"She sounds fun."

"She was. Again, I can't believe my parents hired a fifteen-year-old to watch us. Cheap labor, I guess. I can't imagine letting a child watch Zoe, and fifteen is a child to me now."

"I babysat at that age. Cut ol' Hailey a break. She was brave. I'd actually like to talk to her. She might know or have seen something in connection to Lizzie's abduction that could potentially help us now."

"I haven't seen her since I was…maybe ten? Her parents divorced a few years after they lost her sister to a drowning. It was tragic. Hailey's older brother was watching her, and she fell into the pool and drowned. He had no idea she'd gotten out of the house. She was four. Maybe five. It was hazy. I remember my parents talking about it. How horrifying and unimaginable. Then a year later, Lizzie was gone."

Cars in the drive and a UTV sounded. "The team is here."

Ruby met them at the door and Tanner Ford, Parker Walsh, Dylan Jeong and Brandie Weller entered. Jacqueline stayed with Zoe this morning. Protection detail.

After greetings and everyone grabbing breakfast and coffee, they sat around the table, dogs in resting positions. Lot of dogs in the mix now. He kinda liked it. Could see why Ruby wanted a whole kennel full of them.

"Was the lodge comfortable?" Nick asked.

"Ridge really does snore," Parker said with a grin. "So while the lodge was comfortable, I didn't get a lot of sleep. I don't know how *you* sleep with that going all night," he said to Dylan.

"When you've been on a few tours with bombs going all night, it's like a whisper, dude."

"What did you do in the military?" Nick asked Dylan.

"Helicopter pilot."

"CID."

They exchanged understanding nods and smiles.

Ruby stood. "Let's get the ball rolling. What do we know from yesterday?"

Tanner went to the whiteboard, his boxer, Britta, following. He took a dry-erase marker. "Jeremy Benedict may have called in sick the past three days, but I don't think he truly was. We followed the money and talked to friends and according to one—Billy Thomas—he wanted a long weekend of fishing. His debit-card purchases lean toward this. Fishing gear. A new pole. Camping stuff. He also rented a camping spot, tent camping, near the Rainbow Loop. What was interesting to me, though, is Billy said Jeremy had been unhappy at Lake Chelan and was planning to talk to you about seeing if he could get his old trail guide job back and maybe a spot for Billy, too."

Ruby cocked her head. "He say why?"

"No. Just liked working for Nick compared to the two managers he'd previously worked for, and he really didn't like Luca Hattaway."

Nick grinned. "Nice to know. But he never approached or called me. I had no idea."

"According to employees at Lake Chelan Stables, neither did they. Other than he asked for a raise and it was denied. They're on hold with raises right now, which tells me they aren't doing as well financially as they want to be. I wonder if your success is stealing business from them indirectly. And if so, they might have hidden grudges," Tanner said and made notes on the board.

Dear Reader,

Your opinions are important to us. So if you'll participate in our fast and free "One Minute" Survey, YOU can pick up to four wonderful books that WE pay for when you try the Harlequin Reader Service!

As a leading publisher of women's fiction, we'd love to hear from you. That's why we promise to reward you for completing our survey.

IMPORTANT: Please complete the survey and return it. We'll send your Free Books and a Free Mystery Gift right away. And we pay for shipping and handling too! *We pay for EVERYTHING!*

Try **Love Inspired® Romance Larger-Print** and get 2 books and fall in love with inspirational romances that take you on an uplifting journey of faith, forgiveness and hope.

Try **Love Inspired® Suspense Larger-Print** and get 2 books where courage and optimism unite in stories of faith and love in the face of danger.

Or TRY BOTH!

Thank you again for participating in our "One Minute" Survey. It really takes just a minute (or less) to complete the survey… and your free books and gift will be well worth it!

If you continue with your subscription, you can look forward to curated monthly shipments of brand-new books from your selected series, always at a discount off the cover price! Plus you can cancel any time. So don't miss out, return your One Minute Survey today to get your Free books.

Pam Powers

"One Minute" Survey

GET YOUR FREE BOOKS AND A FREE GIFT!

✓ Complete this Survey ✓ Return this survey

1 Do you try to find time read every day?

☐ YES ☐ NO

2 Do you prefer books which reflect Christian values?

☐ YES ☐ NO

3 Do you enjoy having books delivered to your home?

☐ YES ☐ NO

4 Do you find a Larger Print size easier on your eyes?

☐ YES ☐ NO

YES! I have completed the above "One Minute" Survey. Please send me my Free Books and a Free Mystery Gift (worth over $20 retail). I understand that I am under no obligation to buy anything, as explained on the back of this card.

☐ **Love Inspired® Romance Larger-Print**
122/322 CTI G29C

☐ **Love Inspired® Suspense Larger-Print**
107/307 CTI G29C

☐ **BOTH**
122/322 & 107/307 CTI G29E

FIRST NAME	LAST NAME

ADDRESS

APT.#	CITY

STATE/PROV.	ZIP/POSTAL CODE

EMAIL ☐ Please check this box if you would like to receive newsletters and promotional emails from Harlequin Enterprises ULC and its affiliates. You can unsubscribe anytime.

HARLEQUIN Reader Service — **Here's how it works:**

Accepting your 2 free books and free gift (gift valued at approximately $10.00 retail) places you under no obligation to buy anything. You may keep the books and gift and return the shipping statement marked "cancel." If you do not cancel, approximately one month later we'll send you 6 more books from each series you have chosen, and bill you at our low, subscribers-only discount price. Love Inspired® Romance Larger-Print books and Love Inspired® Suspense Larger-Print books consist of 6 books each month and cost just $6.49 each in the U.S. or $6.74 each in Canada. That is a savings of at least 13% off the cover price. It's quite a bargain! Shipping and handling is just 50¢ per book in the U.S. and $1.25 per book in Canada*. You may return any shipment at our expense and cancel at any time by contacting customer service — or you may continue to receive monthly shipments at our low, subscribers-only discount price plus shipping and handling.

▲ If offer card is missing write to: Harlequin Reader Service, P.O. Box 1341, Buffalo, NY 14240-8531 or visit www.ReaderService.com ▲

BUSINESS REPLY MAIL
FIRST-CLASS MAIL PERMIT NO. 717 BUFFALO, NY

POSTAGE WILL BE PAID BY ADDRESSEE

HARLEQUIN READER SERVICE
PO BOX 1341
BUFFALO NY 14240-8571

NO POSTAGE
NECESSARY
IF MAILED
IN THE
UNITED STATES

"Therefore sabotaging you so you'd fail might garner them more business."

"They found Jeremy close to your property," Ruby said. "Could he have been coming to talk to you? Hiking so no one would notice his vehicle and put two and two together. If you said no, and Lake Chelan Stables got wind, they might let him go, especially if he knew they weren't doing well financially. Then he'd have exhausted the outfitters since he's worked at all of them."

Nick nodded. "It's possible. His place isn't but about two miles away from me."

"So was he in on the kidnapping, things went sideways and he was killed? Or was he close by coming to ask about a job and maybe saw something he shouldn't? Maybe he was in on it and had second thoughts because he liked you. He was coming to warn you and maybe even ask for a job back, too. We need check and see if we can connect him to Aaron Millsap. Tanner, Parker? You two run that angle and work with Jasmin. She can work her well-oiled fingers on the tech side."

Tanner nodded and told them the other two outfitters seemed to be a bust. If they were hurting financially, it hadn't been brought to their attention, but Jasmin was looking into their public records. She'd have something for them later today.

"And did you talk to Yolanda Martin and Priscilla Overton?"

Parker grinned. "They were conveniently off for a long weekend and won't be back until late tonight. Both are scheduled to work tomorrow. But Jasmin couldn't find a connection between either of them and Aaron Millsap, the ex-con Nick had put away." Didn't mean there wasn't one.

Ruby nodded. "Good work. Maybe take a trip over there before dark and see if they're back. Be a welcome mat for them."

Tanner chuckled. "Will do."

Ruby ran her teeth across her bottom lip. "Nick…"

He knew where this was going. Brandie Weller was going to work the cold case on Lizzie. It was now her turn to present her findings.

Nick braced himself and nodded for Ruby to continue the debriefing.

Brandie cleared her throat and gave Nick an apologetic smile. Ruby had the urge to toss her the lint roller; her pants were covered in dog hair. Her dog, Taz, stayed at his post while she came to the board.

"I requested the files from the park rangers who investigated all those years ago and contacted the lead agent and the local detective. They remembered the case because it was a stumper." Her loose ponytail swung as she turned toward the board and wrote Lizzie's name. "They still, sadly, believe she was abducted and—" she glanced at Nick "—and perished. It's possible she was taken onto a shuttle bus to the ferry. No one would have asked questions, especially twenty-five years ago, and the security wasn't as beefed up as now. And that's if she made it out of the park, which they don't believe she did."

Ruby's stomach knotted as she stole a peek at Nick. His face had blanched, and he swallowed hard. He already knew this information, but it was never easy to rehash. "Is there anyone at all from their neighborhood, work, et cetera, who had an interest in Lizzie? Nothing stood out to anyone?"

"A woman who'd been in the bathroom said another

woman had been hovering. She noticed her standing at the door, holding a bunch of brochures on the park, and thought she might be waiting on someone, but she seemed sketchy to her. It was a fleeting thought, one she forgot until the news went out that a little girl had gone missing. That jogged her memory and she called the park rangers. We have her description and a picture a sketch artist drew. They circulated the picture, and a few other women who had been at the park that day called in and recognized her. Said she'd been at the bathrooms and someone saw her wandering around the kiddie horse rides. No one saw her with a child of her own or another person. But they never identified her or found her. So…it went cold."

This piece of information must be what gave Nick hope that Lizzie might still be alive. If this woman stole her and took her on a ferry, maybe she was alive. Somewhere. But she feared that wasn't the case. Rarely did these kinds of abductions turn out with a happy ending. Families had to figure out a way to keep moving on and fight through the grief and uncertainty. Ruby couldn't imagine doing that without her faith. Some days peace was hard enough to have knowing the Lord. Without Him, there would be no real chance at all. Nothing lasting.

She sure needed some peace today. She had a big responsibility and desperately wanted to catch whoever had tried to kidnap Zoe, and kill them. There were a lot of pieces to this puzzle. She could barely find an edge piece. But Mama had taught her to never quit, never throw in the towel. She'd taught her how to dig in her heels and get the job done and to do it right. To do it to the glory of God and trust that each day His grace would be sufficient. It always had been sufficient for Mama, even if she was worn slap-out. They'd always had food on the table, if meager at times, and clothes on their backs, if a bit thin, and a roof over their heads even if it sagged some and occasionally leaked in the bathroom.

God, I need Your grace. We need Your grace.

She called their tech analyst, Jasmin, and put her on speaker for Brandie and Nick to hear, too. She answered on the first ring. "Hey, Ruby."

"Hey. Where are we on the woman who might have been distracting Nick the day Zoe had been abducted?"

"I was able to get some digital photos of the Labor Day festival from the cloud, since any photo a person takes that is marked public goes into the digital-storage cloud bank as public domain." Keys clacked on a keyboard.

"Okay, so I put in the date and location and there are quite a few people snapping photos. I've been surfing them to see if I can find Nick or Zoe. Also some of the stuff in there…just no. Anyway, I'm sifting through them now… Hold on—hold on," she said with more excitement. "Just found a shot of a little boy near Nick and the lady who distracted him in the background! She's a complete likeness of the sketch the artist sent me. Good job, Mr. Rossi, on your description. I'm going to email it to you, but I know the Wi-Fi is shoddy there."

"We can get limited access at the Stehekin Lodge," Nick said.

"Great." This might be a break for them. "Can we have them printed? Circulate them? Or at least download it to our phones at the lodge and show it around. Someone might be able to identify her. Jasmin, send the photo through all federal databases. See if she turns up using face recognition."

"You got it."

"Thanks, girl. You rock." She ended the call, and the phone rang again. She recognized the number. "It's the chief." She answered, but didn't put it on speaker. Nick might be helping but he wasn't privy to all their knowledge. He was, after all, a civilian. "Hey, Chief."

"Ruby. We're having a video call at eleven hundred hours. We have a lead on the stolen bloodhound puppies. Can you get to Wi-Fi out there?"

"Yeah. A lodge nearby has limited access. I'm so glad to hear there's a new lead on the pups."

"Me, too. See you all then."

Chief was always quick about his words.

"We have an eleven-o'clock video chat," Ruby said. "We can download the photo while we're at the lodge."

"Lead on the stolen pups?" Brandie asked.

Ruby nodded. Those poor babies. She hoped whoever had lifted them were at least treating them well. Feeding and watering them and showing love and kindness. The team had speculated about why they'd been stolen— for simply the resale value or because of their excellent scent-detection capabilities, but why? How would a thief utilize those skills? Chief, Ranger and Agent hadn't even been trained in detection when they were stolen; lead trainer Peyton Burns had been doing basic training and acclimating them to the national parks and the terrain. Nothing about the theft made much sense. She said a silent prayer for them, their safety and that they'd be returned unharmed.

Ruby, Tanner, Parker, Dylan and Brandie crammed in around the laptop they'd set up in a small conference room at Stehekin Lodge. One by one, the PNK9 agents popped on the Zoom screen and they chatted while waiting on the chief to arrive.

Finally, he did.

"Thank you all for being prompt. I know you have mountains of work to do."

"Nice pun," Dylan said and nudged Brandie with his elbow. She snickered, but then sobered up. She really wanted the job with the PNK9 unit. Ruby also wanted to chat privately about the Lizzie Rossi cold case and if Brandie had any leads, personally, but hadn't had an opportunity. Nick was with Zoe right now, so after the meeting, she would talk with her.

"Real funny," the chief said with a smirk. "I have some news. A possible lead on the puppies. An anonymous tip came in that they had been spotted near Big Four Mountain Ice Caves and that they might be hiding inside."

"You don't buy that, do you?" Ruby asked. The caves were basically shaped by melting snow, waterfalls from the cliff and the wind.

"Who is going to keep puppies or hang out in a dangerous snow cave?" Parker asked.

"Underneath an avalanche waiting to happen," Ruby added. She quickly did the math. The ferry ride to Field's Landing Point was four hours, then it was another trek to Granite Falls.

"I'll have to fly whoever can go out," Dylan said. "Twenty-five minutes by plane. I see you doing the math in your head," he added with a grin.

"What time do we rendezvous?" Ruby asked.

"Four. Before it gets too dark. It's already dangerous enough." The chief's voice was grim. "I'll be coming, too. Not going to ask any of you to do something I wouldn't. I've cleared it with the rangers in the jurisdiction. We're good to go and they're on standby if we need backup, or, hopefully not, medical aid."

Signs were posted everywhere not to to go inside the caves, which were ever-shifting and dangerous. People had been killed in there before. This was either another false lead with hopes to trap them, or someone was just foolish enough to hide there because no one with half a brain would go spelunking in Four Caves. But if they could get the puppies back, what other option did they have?

"Tanner," the chief added, "Asher will be picking you up for another mission."

"You don't want me to go to the caves?"

Asher Gilmore's face filled the screen. "We're going to the Stark Mountain Lodge in the North Cascades. To visit Eli Ballard."

Ruby's head swam and her stomach roiled. Eli. She hadn't seen him since her breakup text. Her mouth turned dry, and she worked to keep a stoic face, to give nothing away. The team had rallied around her and claimed he'd fooled all of them with his charismatic ways, but Ruby still felt guilty and shaky on good-judgment grounds.

"Are we bringing up the fact that we know Eli was at your dad's nursing home and that he took a photo of your father?" Tanner asked. The photo was what Eli might have used to blackmail Mara with—to stay silent about *him* being the real killer of Stacey Stark and Jonas Digby.

"No, on good chance he is framing Mara for the murders," Asher said. "It's the only logical reason for Mara to go underground. And we don't want to make Eli run before we have enough evidence to bring him in."

Asher had maintained Mara's innocence since she'd been found standing over Stacey and Jonas's dead bodies, then gone on the run. Even though Asher and Mara had never been close, he believed in his gut—and heart—that his half sister wasn't a killer and couldn't have committed the murders. Now, with Eli in the mix, the strong possibility that she *had* been framed gave them all hope.

"Then let's get moving," the chief said. "Everyone be safe."

Easier said than done. They had danger coming at them from every side and now they were knowingly walking into faulty ice caves that could impale them with ice or trap them or crush them. On top of everything else going on.

Ruby felt far from safe.

NINE

Ruby and the team hiked the two miles that led to the ice caves below Big Four Mountain. The caves could only be seen between the summer months, but the shade from the north side meant they were never fully without ice and snow. The sound of the waterfall was powerful and would be peaceful if it wasn't for the fact that they were going inside caves that should never be entered.

Which meant whoever had the puppies was foolish and likely not caring or considerate of the pups. That gave Ruby more determination to go in and find them, return them to safety and get them out of the hands of the jerks who stole them.

From the slippery rocks and lush vegetation, Ruby spotted the entrances into the caves. She'd donned her PNK9 jacket like the rest of the team, but it wasn't terribly cold. At least, not out here in the warm September weather. But the hint of a chill could be felt from the capped mountains, and inside the cave, the temperature would drop considerably.

Chief Fanelli rallied the troops. "Ruby, you take lead. Jackson, Brandie and Dylan in the center tunnel with Ruby." He then made three more groups, one led by Tanner, one by Isaac and the other by him. "We won't have signal with our cells or satellite phones. Stay close." He prayed and then they headed for their designated cave tunnels.

As they neared the entrance, they moved at a slow pace to keep from sliding on slippery rocks; the terrain became more rugged as the trail ended. The fact that the bridge was out of commission worked in their favor. No tourists, and average hikers wouldn't dare attempt to use the treacherous routes to arrive here.

"Who do you think the anonymous tip came from?" Brandie asked.

"The puppy nappers themselves, if you ask me," Dylan answered from behind her. Brandie slipped and Ruby turned as she heard it, but Dylan had already broken her fall. Brandie's cheeks turned pink, and not from the hike.

"Thanks," she said breathlessly.

"Anytime," he returned.

Ruby filed the scene away to ask about later. "Everybody good?"

Jackson Dean brought up the rear. "All good back here, boss."

Ruby rolled her eyes. "Do not call me *boss*. By the way, that bear spray Everly gave me? Came in handy yesterday. Mine wasn't on my belt." Jackson and the woman he was seriously dating, Everly, had reconnetcted during a dangerous case in Olympic National Park, where Everly had been studying and tracking bears.

"The grizz get ya?" he asked.

"No-o-o. Because of the *bear spray*. And it was a black bear."

Everyone chuckled as they pushed on, the temperature dropping as they approached the caves. They paused. The silence hung heavy in the air. Finally, Ruby turned. "We go slow and steady."

Dylan pulled a piece of wool blanket from his backpack. "Peyton gave me this. It has the puppies' scent on it." Peyton had been training the pups and was taking the theft harder than anyone.

Dylan let Ridge get the scent, then held it out to Ruby. She let Pepper sniff. Jackson's Doberman was trained in protection. Brandie's German shepherd, Taz, was cross-trained and he scented on the blanket as well. Between all their canines, if the bloodhounds were in the cave, they were going to be found.

"Track, Pepper, but easy. Easy." She needed the Lab to go slow. They crept into the chilly cave, Ruby's flashlight beam casting eerie shadows. The rubble and ice made for slippery walkways. The sound of cracking overhead gave Ruby the shivers.

The four teams fanned out, carefully maneuvering. The cave was long and wide, but as they moved farther back, it began to branch off into tunnels. Each team took one and the icy walls narrowed until they were moving single file, including the dogs.

"Do dogs get claustrophobia?" Dylan asked.

"How can you be a dog handler and not know this?" Ruby countered with a teasing tone and followed Pepper, who was up about fifteen feet on the leash, Ridge right beside her and Dylan now behind Ruby.

"Yeah," Brandie said, razzing him, too, "how can you not know this? Of course, they can be. If they've ever been confined under duress."

Pepper had a scent and Ridge, too. Brandie's German shepherd was trying to move past them, and Brandie called him to slow and follow. He obeyed. Ruby wasn't sure what scent they had. None had alerted yet.

The cave continued to creak and pop overhead and

Ruby's chest constricted, her nerves taut. The narrow passage widened until they were in a cavern, and suddenly Pepper, Ridge and Taz sat, alerting.

"The puppies are here," Brandie said and rubbed Taz's head. "Good boy."

Or they *were*. Ruby shined her light. It appeared someone had been in the cave. There were a few empty beer cans and a couple of chip bags. Pepper whimpered and Ruby whispered, "Track." Pepper hurried to a huge boulder and sat. Next to it was an old blanket. Pepper sat right beside it. "Blanket. Looks identical to the one we had at the training center where the bloodhounds had been taken. Like the piece Peyton gave you, Dylan."

Jackson approached and surveyed the area. "Has dog hair on it, too." He bagged it and then he and Dylan collected the cans and chip bags as evidence for prints at the very least. Once everything was bagged and put into backpacks, Ruby made the call to leave.

"I wonder if the other teams have had any success?" Brandie asked.

"I don't know. The only other channel to move through is a crevice barely big enough for me. I don't see anyone taking puppies through it. I think we should get out of—"

A ripping and cracking sent Ruby's heart into her throat as a mountainous piece of ice fell from the ceiling. Ruby shrieked, jumping out of the way in the nick of time. "Now. Let's go now. Quickly but carefully."

A foot ahead, Pepper circled and alerted again.

Ruby tiptoed over and shined her light. "Oh, boy." Lying in snow, it was almost invisible. "That's a kilo of cocaine or maybe heroin."

"Do you think it connects with whoever stole the pups?" Jackson asked.

Ruby couldn't be sure. "Can't say for certain but it has our bloodhounds' scent, or Pepper wouldn't have alerted. I doubt it was left here on purpose. Someone might have been counting it or weighing it, set it down and didn't realize it was missing since it blended in with the snow. But I can say it's worth a lot of money. Enough that they won't miss it for long and they will come back for it."

"Hey, this was beside it," Dylan said and retrieved a crumbled piece of paper with a sticky red stain.

"Is that blood?" Brandie asked.

"I don't think so. Looks more like red fruit punch or something," Dylan said.

The echo of snow splitting sent a chill down Ruby's spine. "Let's bag it all and figure it out later. I want out of this place."

Jackson bagged the drugs and the crumpled paper separately. "Hey..." He shined his light on the paper. "There's little pieces of black dog hair on this stain. And a little of the red is on the plastic of the drugs, too."

So someone must have been drinking a red drink and spilled it. Which is why they missed picking up the kilo. Why would drug runners want bloodhound puppies? "We'll know more once the lab runs trace evidence. Let's get out of—"

A gunshot cracked and a bullet narrowly missed Ruby and slammed into the ice wall, which cracked. Tiny fissures branched in multiple directions, fanning out like roads on a map, the sound as deafening as the echo of the gunfire. Ruby's ears rang and they all crouched.

"Must have come from that back tunnel. Move!" Dylan said.

They were in the open, and their dogs were in danger. Several more bullets whizzed by. Whoever was shooting was putting themselves in danger, too. The bullets slamming into ice and snow could cause an avalanche and crush all of them, including the shooter.

Unless he was hiding near a spot that opened up to the hiking trails, which someone who was used to taking risks and had been in this cave many times might know.

"Ambush!" Jackson hollered and they began rushing single-file toward the base of the cave, out of the cavern and through the narrow passage. The walls quaked and more gunfire sounded, but the bullets were hitting walls. On purpose?

The horrific sound of ripping echoed and Ruby squealed as a huge chunk of ice fell, blocking not only the width of the tunnel, but also almost right to the top, leaving about a two-foot margin overhead. "We got real trouble here," she said. Her heart pounded and sweat slicked her spine. They were pinned in. She and Brandie might be able to slide on their bellies across the barrier and over to the other side, but Dylan and Jackson would never make it. They were too big. Ridge would never fit, and she was fairly sure Taz was too big as well.

How were they going to move a solid block of ice? It was like moving granite.

From afar, the sound of more gunfire erupted.

The other teams.

They were all being targeted.

Another round of gunshots let loose and Ruby winced and prayed the rest of their team was unharmed. What if they were being picked off one by one? "We have to get over this ice. Help the others. Let them know we're stuck. We can't go back. We have shooters in the tunnel."

"Who might now know we have their drugs. Maybe they were coming back for it and saw us," Brandie said.

"You may be right. Look. Let's hoist Brandie up. She can slide over the hunk of ice to the other side and get help. The rest of us will stay and…" Fight to the death? "And figure it out."

"Taz won't fit, and I'm not leaving him. Ruby, you go. Pepper will fit."

Ruby didn't want to leave her colleagues. "I need to stay with the team."

"No," Dylan said. "Brandie's right. Taz might get anxious without her, anyway, and we don't have the same bond with him as she does. You and Pepper go. We got this."

Ruby hated to leave her team. It felt like abandoning them. But she knew it was best and arguing wasn't going to help anyone. "Hoist me up."

She stepped into Dylan's hands and he and Jackson helped her onto the large chunk of ice, the chill quickly seeping into her uniform. She lay flat on her stomach, shivering, and scooted sideways and forward. "Come on, girl. It's okay," she said softly, but blood whooshed in her head and her heart thumped against her rib cage.

Jackson and Dylan helped Pepper onto the ice and she crawled to Ruby. "That's it. Good girl." They'd been in tight spaces before. Never on ice, though. But Pepper handled it like a champ.

There was no easy way to slide off and it wasn't far down, but she didn't land gracefully. She helped Pepper down and they headed toward the larger cavern, where they'd entered. As she turned a corner, she smacked right into a hard chest and kneed her assailant, then struck his chin.

"Ah! Whoa! It's me," Isaac McDane said through a grunt in a tight voice. "Nice defense moves, though," he added as he let out a slow painful breath.

"Sorry. Where's your group?"

"Everyone is out. The chief and I came back in to find you guys. Where's your group?"

"Trapped. Behind a thick wall of ice that fell. But they're okay. Not for long, unless the shooters got smart and out of Dodge. About a hundred feet back. It's wedged good. We need heat. Something to melt it down and get them out." But she knew even saying it that bringing in heat to a snow cave was signing a death warrant. While it melted the ice, it would also melt walls and could cause an avalanche.

"Let's relay the news. Then we get in there and we get our team out." His looming frame cast shadows and his intense blue eyes bore into hers. "We will get them out."

She nodded and followed him out, which was no easy feat. The rocks were slippery and they were cautious of who might still be inside. Finally, almost twenty minutes later, they emerged from the cave.

Chief spotted them and ran for them. "Thank You, God! You guys are safe."

The snow shook. And the sound of something massive breaking loose rattled her eardrums. The snowcap rumbled and shook, gaining momentum.

Ruby stood in horror as the avalanche roared and covered the entrances.

"Chief," Ruby said through a cracking voice and tears. "The team's still inside."

Nick raced out the front door of his cabin as the PNK9 SUV pulled into his driveway. Ruby barely got out of the car before he had her in his arms. He couldn't care less that there were onlookers. When Jacqueline got news that the team had been fired on and then an avalanche had covered the cave entrances where they'd been looking for the bloodhound pups, trapping the team, he was beside himself.

Ruby was hesitant to embrace him, but he felt her arms loosely come around his waist. "I was scared to death," he said.

She broke away and put distance between them. "We're okay. I'm sorry we scared you." So formal. "The team found a side tunnel that led out to the west side of the cave into the hiking trails. Probably the same one the shooters used to flee. They were out when the avalanche happened. Of course, we didn't know that. They had to hike around the caves to get back to us and the signal on the satellite phone wasn't working."

He looked up at the team members who'd been with her—Brandie and Dylan. Parker and Jacqueline blew out of the house, Jacqueline nearly knocking Ruby down with a hug. Ruby clung to her and when Jacqueline whispered in her ear, Ruby nodded then hugged her even tighter. They were good friends and had known each other for years, but he felt a twinge of green. He shouldn't have expected anything but professionalism from Ruby. But they'd been sharing a lot of personal things and he thought there might be a connection between them, if only friendship. Romance wasn't on his radar right now. Bigger fish to fry and all, but he'd expected something besides cold professionalism.

"Come inside. I made coffee and we have food. I imagine you're all hungry and wiped out."

"That we are," Dylan said. "And we appreciate the offer, but we're going to head to the lodge and get some rest." He shook Nick's hand and Parker did as well.

"I'm glad none of you were hurt," Parker said. "I wish I could have been there."

"You were needed here as Jacqueline's backup," Ruby said. "I appreciate that you stayed."

"When Ruby gets a chance," Dylan said, "ask her about her ice-rock-climbing skills." He grinned and then he and Parker returned to the vehicle with their dogs. "We'll be back in the morning."

She nodded. "See you tomorrow."

"I'm pretty beat, too," Brandie said. "I think I'll head out, too. You know the saying—'princesses only wake up pretty if they get beauty sleep.'"

"No," Ruby said. "Can't say I do." She laughed and headed inside.

Nick shrugged. Seemed like he'd heard it before but couldn't say where.

Inside, Jacqueline retired, leaving only him and Ruby in the kitchen. "Can I make you something to eat?"

"I'm starving, thanks."

She collapsed into one of the kitchen chairs and he paused before making her a sandwich. He came to the table. "I'm sorry. I shouldn't have done that out there. Hugged you like that. I apologize for my lack of professionalism."

Ruby's eyes shone and she swiped them and stood. "Nick… I'm sorry. It's just the guy I was recently involved with… I can't have my team members thinking I'm repeating history. Not that you might be a bad guy, but… I've resolved not to date men on cases I'm working."

Ah. He understood but felt a dull thump in his chest.

"I understand. And I *am* sorry for embarrassing you, but I'm not sorry for caring about you or for your safety." He moved in closer. "I do care about you, Ruby. I know it's only been a few days, but I admire you. You're brave and resilient, tough but kind. I'm not sure I've met anyone like you before."

Her bottom lip trembled. "I'm glad we met, too. And it wasn't that I didn't want the hug. I could use one."

"Is that an invitation?"

"I thought I lost good friends today," she said, her voice croaking. "So yeah. It is."

In one stride, he had her in his arms, wrapped against him, her head on his chest. "I know what that feels like. And I know what it feels like to actually lose friends." He'd seen too many killed in war.

"I felt like I abandoned them." She shared how she climbed a chunk of ice to find help and how the avalanche struck so fast. "There I was watching and knowing I should have been inside with them. I was their team leader. Even after we discovered they'd gotten out and hugged it out, I still felt guilty."

He stroked her hair and let his chin rest on the top of her head. "I understand," he murmured. "But they knew the risks. All of you knew the possibilities going in. Knew the outcome might not be a hopeful one. No one blames you, Ruby."

"I know. I blame me. For so much. For not being enough for my dad to want me, for not being wise in choosing relationships, for being duped by men who..." She leaned her head back, looking up into his eyes. Her warm brown-eyed gaze latched onto his. "I shouldn't be unloading on you like this. I feel like..."

Like it was easy. Like they'd been this way for years, known each other a lifetime. Been in this embrace a million times before. No, she wasn't looking for romance. And he wasn't, either. But they had built a foundation of friendship. "Like what?" He wanted to hear the rest of her sentence. Wanted to know if she felt what he was feeling, which, if he admitted it to himself, might be more than friendship.

Her top teeth scraped across her full bottom lip and she sighed. "It doesn't matter. My feelings aren't always fact. And I can't trust them. I'm sorry." She slipped from his embrace. "I appreciate the offer for food, but suddenly, I'm more tired than hungry. I'm gonna go to bed. But thanks. Really."

Before he had time to object or ask more questions or offer her the kitchen without his presence to distract her, she was hustling up the stairs, Pepper right behind. "Good night," he muttered and pinched the bridge of his nose.

This was probably the best, anyway.

Lord, why am I feeling like this? Why so sudden and intense? Maybe he couldn't trust his feelings, either. He needed wisdom and discernment, big-time.

Bone-weary, he slogged to his bedroom, grabbed his pillow and headed for Zoe's floor, where he'd made a pallet at the foot of her bed and slept with one eye and ear open since that first frightening day. She slept soundly, peacefully. He thanked God for the gift of people who could protect her and make her feel safe. Every good and perfect gift came from Him. This was good.

Now if only God would give them the gift of finding the kidnapper who was also responsible for trying to murder them.

TEN

Ruby awoke, startled from a strange dream.

It was 2:07 a.m.

The dream replayed in her mind, fresh and vivid. She'd been left on the same ledge that Zoe had been on. She was all alone and frightened. Her father showed up, and she was happy to see him. Thankful he'd come for her and not abandoned her after all. The love in her heart and the warmth she felt at him appearing was something she'd never have wanted to wake up from.

But then, when she reached out to him, he ignored her hand. Didn't reach back. When she called, he looked away. The ledge began to crumble and below was nothing but jagged rocks emerging from the drowning depths.

The warmth and love she'd felt instantly chilled and left her hollow and terrified. She couldn't move. And the ledge continued to quake and tear in two until she was falling, falling…her dad long gone. Vanished. He'd seemingly arrived to save her, to rescue her and to love her, but he'd refused.

She was unwanted. Unloved. Abandoned. And struck down, falling to her death below. As she hit the sharp boulders, she'd jerked awake. Sweat-laden, with her pulse racing, she untangled herself from the sheets. Jacqueline slept next to her like a hibernating bear.

Ruby padded in her cotton pants and T-shirt to the bathroom and splashed cool water on her flushed face. It was just a dream. No, a nightmare. But it had felt so real. The emotions were real. Her dad had never cared about her. Only himself. Unlike Nick, who had not only reached out for his child but also climbed down into the danger to be with her. To pull her into his arms, reassure her that she was okay. That he was with her. She was safe.

She toweled her damp face and blew a heavy sigh. Her stomach rumbled. She hadn't eaten since lunch yesterday afternoon and could use some sustenance. A cup of tea. If she was quiet, she wouldn't wake anyone downstairs. As she entered the kitchen, the earlier embrace she'd shared with Nick circled back. She'd didn't want to think about it, but it was a far better scenario to ruminate on than the horrific nightmare.

She'd been hugged by men before—men she'd even had romantic relationships with—but none of them, not even Eli, had felt like Nick's hold around her. It wasn't possessive or selfish. But generous and safe. A place she knew she could be herself and reveal the most hurtful truths and insecurities, but she'd refrained.

When he'd raced to her after the avalanche, she'd felt like a princess being rescued from a castle. Cared for in a way she never had before. She wanted to latch on and not let go, but then the shame of falling for Eli and who he might be came full force, and the last thing she wanted was for her team to think she fell for every single man she came within twenty feet of. Though she'd never dated anyone involved in a case before Eli, the blunder was humiliating.

No one had said anything about Nick to her, or even given her a side-eye. Even so, she'd pulled away to show professionalism, but it had been with great reluctance. She certainly hadn't meant to offend him or hurt him. Then hearing those words—words no man had ever said. Oh, she'd heard she was pretty, or even gorgeous, from Eli.

But Nick had dug deeper, past the superficial to traits she wasn't even sure she had. He'd found substance and praised her for it. It was far more moving than Eli's empty flattery.

He'd found substance because he was a man of substance. And she'd never experienced that romantically. She couldn't deny that the men in PNK9 were totally stand-up guys, men of honor and noble. But she'd never dated any of them. They felt more like brothers.

This was something different. Or—or maybe she was caught up in the fact that he hadn't flattered her physically. She had herself completely confused. A noise outside caught her attention, and Pepper went on alert. The windows were boarded, so she couldn't see outside. She raced back upstairs and quietly grabbed her gun and mini Maglite, then headed back down to check it out. After slipping out the front door, she edged around the side of the house.

It was eerily quiet, with only the sounds of a distant waterfall. Not even the horses stirred in the stable. She shined her light and caught a shadow.

It moved.

Her heart lurched into her throat, and she aimed the light in the direction of the shadow near the corner of the house by Zoe's bedroom. A dark figure loomed.

"Freeze!"

The shadow bolted, heading for the stables. Behind

them was safety in the thick woods. She'd likely never find him, especially if he was familiar with the terrain. She caught up with the figure near the stables and dove onto the mysterious figure, but the person reared back and elbowed her in the sternum, stealing her breath and sending a shooting pain through her ribs.

It gave her assailant enough time to jump up and bolt again.

"Ruby!"

Nick's voice was in the distance, but she'd lost her breath. The trespasser escaped into the trees. Nick caught up with her, gun in hand. He kneeled. "Hey. Are you okay?"

Her breath returned with a huge gasp and she nodded, then gulped in air. "Yeah. I heard something and went to check it out—"

"Without backup?" He was irritated. "You should know better than that."

She did not need a lecture. But he wasn't wrong. She should have woken Jacqueline, but she hadn't. No excuses for her stupidity. Thankfully, nothing worse happened. "You're right. I'm not going to argue."

He helped her up. "I didn't mean to scold you. Well… yeah, I did." He smirked. "We all know these people— and we're assuming more than one—are dangerous. You could have been ambushed. Promise me you won't do something like this again unless you have no other alternative."

She promised. "Whoever it was, he or she was prowling around Zoe's window."

"I know. I woke to do my shift of a perimeter check. Heard something."

"We probably caught the person before they attempted to mess with the window. They surely know she has a dog and dogs hear everything." She had to wonder what kind of person they were dealing with. A savvy kidnapper would know not to attempt a kidnapping when officers with dogs were in the house. Unless they were planning to incapacitate the dogs. The thought sent a wave of nausea through her stomach.

"What were you doing up so late?" he asked.

"Bad dream. I get them sometimes." Not like this one, though. "Let's sweep the house and make sure everything is secure."

"Agreed."

After checking everything out and pronouncing it clear, they came back inside. It was nearing 3:00 a.m. "You had a bad dream...woke and heard something?"

Her stomach rumbled.

He grinned. "Ah. You came down for food and heard a noise. How about that sandwich?"

"I'm not going to say no." She grinned and he motioned for her to have a seat. He turned on the overhead light and dimmed it, then went to work on a turkey sandwich. Ruby's mouth watered just thinking about the deliciousness.

"Milk or iced tea?"

"Milk. I don't need any caffeine. And y'all don't make it sweet enough, anyway." She wasn't sure she would be able to return to slumber. She was wide-eyed.

After handing her a sandwich loaded with turkey, cheese, lettuce, tomatoes and mayo, Nick went to work on his own sandwich and joined her at the counter. They ate in comfortable silence for a while.

"I think we might need to consider doing something I originally didn't want to," Nick said.

Ruby's stomach roiled. Was he talking about a date? "What's that?" she whispered.

"Getting Zoe out of here and somewhere safe."

Relief filled her chest, but the thought of Zoe in danger again only brought the nausea back full force. She pushed away her plate. "I agree. We have access to safe houses. Jackson Dean used to be a US Marshal and has connections. I know Jacqueline would go along. Zoe knows her already and feels safe with her."

"I was thinking that same thing, minus the safe house. But that only sweetens the pot."

"It might take a couple of days to get the request and permission. I'll call Jackson at first light. He'll be up. He can coordinate with the chief, and once it's finalized, we'll make the plans to get them safe. In the meantime, we keep doing what we're doing. Take shifts on keeping watch over the house. Between us and Jacqueline, we can get some decent sleep."

"You're an organizer. I like that."

"I learned early to be that way." She finished off her milk and rinsed her glass in the sink. She turned. "Have you given any more thought to going back into some kind of law enforcement after this thing is squashed and everyone is safe?"

"No. No time. I mean, yeah…but no."

She grinned. "You were CID once. You'd make a great park ranger agent, and that keeps you in the park. You could even keep your horse outfitter. Maybe not even have to move if you were granted your request for the North Cascades National Park."

Nick grinned. "I may not have given it a lot of thought, but you certainly have." He rubbed his chin. "An agent with the park rangers. It's not an unattractive idea."

"You have experience with both and being former military only adds to your résumé. I'd give you a personal reference even, or professional as a federal agent myself. I mean, if you want. I sound really pushy here. I'm not trying to be." She laughed and shrugged.

"No, you're not being pushy. Well, you are. In a good way. No one has pushed me in a long time. I guess I let my old dreams fall by the wayside." He rinsed the crumbs from his plate. "I'm not sure I'm ready yet. I may never be."

Ruby understood. "Well, it's something to pray about and I know you're a man of faith. That's evident."

"I am. You pray for me, too."

"I will."

"Let's try to get some sleep before the sun rises," he said.

But they both knew neither of them was going back to sleep. There was too much to think about. Not the future, but what was happening right now.

Maybe she would wake up Jackson, anyway. He'd forgive her. They needed to get the ball rolling. Now.

Two days had passed since someone had been outside Zoe's window. Nick had been on edge and all of their efforts had hit dead ends. One thing he'd noticed was that the PNK9 candidate, Brandie, didn't exactly ignore him, but she skirted around him in a cagey manner. His investigative gut said she was hiding something, and he had to wonder if it was anything new on his sister's case.

Ruby had spent every bedtime with Zoe, reading stories and playing games. Zoe had even put on a puppet show for her. While Zoe didn't show a clinginess toward Jacqueline, as she did with Ruby, she did like Jacqueline very much and she trusted her. When a safe house was secured, knowing Zoe was comfortable with the officer would make it easier on him and Zoe when she had to leave.

They'd make it sound like a grand adventure. But not all red tape could be cut, so they waited. Between the six of them—until Parker Walsh had to leave—they'd been keeping an around-the-clock watch on Zoe and the house, and that may be why the past few days had been quieter than usual.

He walked out to the conference room, where Brandie and Ruby were working. Dylan had gone back to talk with Yolanda Martin and Priscilla Overton.

He waltzed into the conference room and Ruby held a grim expression.

"What's going on?" he asked.

"We're just hitting walls. Still waiting on the prints from the cigarette box. We've circulated Aaron's photo around the valley and no one's recognized him. But he can't hide out for long. I think we may have to canvas campgrounds and there's always the possibility he's hiding at someone's home. We still don't know who the girlfriend is, and we know women were involved—at least one woman."

And they still had no identity on the woman who may have purposely distracted him. They downloaded her photo and had circulated it with Aaron's. No go. A few vendors had recognized her from the event, but she hadn't been with a man or little boy—so in all likelihood, she'd lied about a random dude and his son as her own family. Nick had believed her, because why wouldn't he?

"Hey, were there any other pictures of that man and boy without the woman? If we could confirm she had no connection with them, then it would help us determine if she had nefarious intentions approaching me or not. I haven't heard from her, and I gave her my number. My gut says she has no husband or son."

"I'll check with Jasmin. If she finds any that you're talking about, she'll send them over and we'll have to go back to Stehekin Lodge to download and print them out."

"I know it's not easy staying here. Or working out of Stehekin. It's part of the charm to me…originally. Being away from the time-suck and hustle and bustle of the internet and all the social-media stuff." Nick sat across from Brandie as she twirled her hair. "Any news on my sister's case?"

She jerked her head up, her brown eyes staring into the distance like an elk being invaded in the forest. "Um, well…not really. I did try to contact your old babysitter, Hailey Alan. She got married. So her last name changed."

"Good to hear."

"But she divorced last year and changed it back."

"Oh." Not so good.

"Her husband, Rick Weedmont, said they went through some problems after infertility treatments didn't work and Hailey couldn't come back from it. Hailey filed for divorce and left. He isn't sure where she is now. Occasionally, she'll call him from a random place but as far as he knows she has no permanent residence."

"You can't find her?"

"Nope. Jasmin is searching but it's like she fell off the grid. But that's not really unusual. Rick said she was a bit of a conspiracy theorist. A prepper. She insisted he have a bomb shelter put in and she gardened, and never used social media, cell phones or anything where the government could hurt her, or harmful rays could hurt her. So microwaves were a no-no in their household. She thinks it contributed to their infertility issues."

Wow. That was awful.

"He tried to get her to see someone about her paranoia and for a while she did. Things got a little better and then it took a turn. I asked if she might have ever talked about Lizzie Rossi's kidnapping and he said she had. But just that she lost her baby sister and then the sweet girl she babysat for. Nothing that would make him think she saw anything."

Nick sat in the chair and perched his elbows on his knees. "Have you tried connecting her to Aaron Millsap, just in case?"

"Yes. No connection. Can't connect her to Jeremy Benedict, either."

Frustration ate at him. Tomorrow was the twenty-fifth anniversary of his sister's vanishing. He wanted answers and Zoe safe somewhere else prior to the date. That may be why things were so quiet. They were lying in wait.

But why? That was the big question. The one he had no answer to. "I feel like I'm sitting on my hands." He stood and heaved a sigh.

Ruby looked up. "How about we go back to the park and do another sweep. Find hikers. Go to the visitor center and the campground nearby. Most tourists coming in for that festival stayed at the closest campground. They might have seen something."

"Okay. I'm going stir-crazy."

"I understand. Why don't you pack up some food and get the horses ready? We can ride them to the campgrounds instead of UTVs. You owe me a horseback ride. And when this is finished, I won't be such a newbie when we ride with Zoe."

That idea he liked a lot. The horses would calm him, put him in his element, and he'd be working on his daughter's kidnapping so he wouldn't feel guilty over horseback riding with a lovely woman he cared a lot about.

"I'll get on it. Give me thirty minutes."

"Done." She grinned and waved as he hurried outside and to the stables. It was quiet inside. The team had been on trails today with clients. He heard a voice coming from outside the stable. He wandered over and opened the door.

"I need more time…I know." Candy was pacing and her voice raised with anxiety. "Just give me some more time…There's no need to make threats." She turned and spotted Nick, her face blanching. "I gotta go, babe." She hung up. "Husband stuff," she said through a shaky laugh.

More like lies. "Your husband always threaten you?" Nick knew Candy's husband, Garrett, and threatening didn't fit the bill. Why was she lying and whom had she been talking to?

"Threats like me sleeping on the couch if I work another late night again. He misses me." She shrugged but refused to make eye contact. What a quick liar, too.

"What do you need more time for?" he asked.

She kicked at the ground and shoved her hands into her back jean pockets. "Um…with everything going on here, I hate to leave. More time to stay and help out."

Nick wasn't buying it. Disappointment hit his gut like a cold wet lump. "I don't want to come between you and Garrett. So feel free to leave promptly at five. I can get Joe to stick around later."

"Really, I don't mind."

"But Garrett does. Right?" He narrowed his eyes, forced her to keep eye contact. "That was Garrett?"

She swallowed and squeaked out a yes.

"Then you have to do whatever it takes to make a marriage work." He gave her a resolute nod. "Ruby and I are going into the park to visit campgrounds."

"Any new leads?" she asked.

None he would tell her about. She was being shady and now she was out of the loop. "I'm not at liberty to say. But we'll be taking Maple and Juniper. I'll call Joe, let him know our new arrangement." With that, he headed into the stables and went to work on saddling the easiest horse, Maple, for Ruby, and Juniper, a sweet girl but a bit more intimidating in size than Maple, for himself.

Whom had Candy been talking to? Surely she wouldn't be involved in Zoe's kidnapping or the attempts on his life? What would be the motive? She loved Zoe. Had no kids of her own. And Nick had been good to her. Let her off for all their doctor visits and fertility treatments in Seattle. Between that and now trying to be placed as adoptive parents with an agency, it was probably strapping them financially.

Could she have been the one to lure Zoe away? Zoe would have recognized her, but if she was in disguise, like a wig and big sunglasses, and even padded to look larger, Zoe was only three. She could easily be fooled. Candy would have known things to get Zoe to trust her, too. Like favorite snacks and things about the horses and Nick. Zoe would have felt comfortable. And she would have known how to keep her calm so it wouldn't trigger a seizure. Goldie would have been fine, because while she may have been disguised, her scent would be the same. Familiar. Goldie would have gone right along, no problem.

The cold, wet lump in his gut now hardened like concrete as he led the horses to the office and tied them to a post outside. Inside he made a quick lunch basket, using the same foods they packed for their tourist picnics. Though, he didn't think he was going to eat a bite all day.

Ruby's walk was brisk and purposeful as she entered the cabin. She still had on her PNK9 uniform along with a backpack on. Pepper wore her harness with a small dog backpack attached. Ruby paused and cocked her head. "What's wrong? You look unsettled?"

"I am. I could also say the same for you."

"I am. You go first."

Nick sighed and told her about what he'd just overheard and his thoughts. "Has anyone done a more comprehensive check on Candy?"

Ruby nodded. "We've done a thorough background check on all your employees, except for financial records. There's nothing to indicate Candy knows or is involved with the kidnappers, but your gut should always be listened to. We haven't done a check on Garrett Reynolds. I'll make sure Jasmin does now. We might be able to connect Candy's husband to Aaron Millsap or Jeremy Benedict. Which brings me to my not-so-good news."

Nick wasn't sure he could keep taking the bad without any good. "All right."

"We got the prints back from the cigarette carton at the cabin."

He already knew the answer.

"They belong to Aaron Millsap. He's here, Nick. In Stehekin."

ELEVEN

Ruby had been perched on Maple for the better part of the day. The horse was sweet and seemed to know she was nervous. They'd stopped so the horses and Pepper had plenty of snacks and water and rest. The temperature was a cool seventy-two degrees, but even so, they all needed nourishment and hydration.

She and Nick had tossed out theories and ideas on where Aaron Millsap might be hiding out and they'd covered quite a few campgrounds. So far they hadn't found him, seen a log with his name on it or encountered any hikers, campers or tourists who recognized his face, according to the photos they'd been circulating.

Due to the updated information, Nick had saddled two more horses and Dylan and Brandie were also scouring the park outside Stehekin. As far as Candy Reynolds, Ruby had given Nick's ideas some thought and had gotten Jasmin to do some dirty digging, as Ruby liked to call it. She'd have to cross some lines, but nothing illegal. She also had her searching for anything on Candy's husband, Garrett.

Jackson said that the red tape was almost cut. Zoe would be able to go to a safe house either tonight or tomorrow morning. Jacqueline was ready. The team was ready. Ruby's gut—which she tried to listen to—told her that this anniversary of Lizzie Rossi's disappearance meant something. They had to be ready for another attack or kidnapping, or both.

"Tell me the truth," Nick said. "How do you like horseback riding?"

She grinned. "I like it." She patted Maple, a calm and gentle horse. "You've been a good instructor and great company. I could get used to this." Her cheeks flamed as the words tumbled from her mouth. That had come out entirely wrong.

Or maybe not. If she wasn't on a case and unsure of men anymore, she might like time off horseback riding with Nick, having picnics and enjoying the day. The only thing that would make it better would be Zoe with them. She loved hearing that little girl's laugh. She'd been through so much in her short life, from epilepsy to losing her mom, and yet she was a picture of pure joy and contentment. But she had a very strong, loving father, too. One who shielded her, encouraged her, advocated and protected her. That made all the difference.

Proverbs 30:5 hit her heart. *Every word of God is pure: he is a shield unto them that put their trust in him.* And if all His words were pure and true, then she had to believe that He was most certainly her Heavenly Father, who cared for her, never abandoned her. Protected her and advocated for her.

Knowing this truth should bring her more contentment than wishing for the love of an earthly father. *Lord, help me be content. To find all I need in You alone. You're far better than any father I might have on this earth, no matter how good or how poor one might be.*

Nick grinned as they headed up the trail, the trees

hanging over like a canopy, giving them shade and a reprieve from the sun. "I could, too," he said in a soft tone. "Up ahead is Rainbow Falls. Want to settle in and get a bite? Let the horses and Pepper rest again?"

"Sounds good. I'm hungry."

They found a place to spread a blanket and Nick went to work laying it out. Ruby couldn't stop looking at the two-tiered waterfall that dropped almost four hundred feet, with little tiny rainbows from the spray popping out in the sunshine. A reminder of God's promise. That He could be trusted. That He was faithful. Even when others were not. When others couldn't be trusted.

He always could.

By the time her eyes drifted back to Nick, he'd already laid out the red-and-blue-plaid blanket, opened the basket and arranged their food. Chicken salad, croissants, fruit, cheese and fresh lemonade. "I plan to smash that chicken salad and not even feel shame," Ruby said.

Nick chuckled. "Same."

Their backdrop was the sound of water falling into the basin and birds in the trees. Pepper lapped water from her bowl and had a few doggy cookies, then closed her eyes and drifted off into la-la land. Nick and Ruby fed the horses apples and they'd had a drink from the basin of fresh water.

The day would be perfect, if not for the reason they were here.

Tourists walked and took selfies with one another, laughing and enjoying their day in the sun. It wasn't too crowded, but enough to have space and still people-watch. After two croissants and plenty of fruit and cheese, Ruby sighed. "I need a nap."

"I hear that." He began cleanup and Ruby helped. "I

can't remember the last time I picnicked. I've guided tours and eaten while families enjoyed their time together, but I've never been *on* the blanket. The day Lizzie went missing, we had a picnic that day. It had been a perfect afternoon."

Ruby reached out and grabbed his hand. "I'm sorry. If this brought up bad memories."

"No. It's good memories. I need to lean into the good ones more. I tend to focus on the one memory that was the worst and create terrible scenarios. That's no way to live. You've helped me see that with all your talk about becoming an investigative agent for the parks. It's brought back memories I let die. Don't be sorry. I owe you a thank-you."

"You going to look into it?"

"Maybe. Maybe so." He closed the picnic basket.

Pepper stood, circled and sat. "What is it, girl?" Pepper repeated the action. "She's alerting, Nick. She smells our shooter and kidnapper." With good weather, Pepper could catch a scent about five hundred yards away. So the person was somewhere within fifteen hundred feet of them.

Ruby looked across the park and frowned, then grabbed her backpack and pulled out a photo they had. "Hey, Nick. Is that the woman that distracted you?" She looked just like the photo they'd pulled from the cloud.

"Yeah," he said, already getting to his feet. "I think so."

She was talking with another woman. "Who is she with? Wait a second. Let's watch and see what happens." Ruby held him back from jumping the gun.

"I don't know." He looked at the woman their target was speaking to. "She kind of looks like Candy, but she's dressed like an older woman and with the big dark sunglasses, hat and oversize coat, I can't tell for sure. That's weird, right?"

"Call the office. See if Candy's there." He used his satellite phone and made the call, holding it out for Ruby to hear, too. Joe answered the stable line.

"Hey, Joe, can I talk to Candy?"

He snorted. "I wish. She bolted right after you left. Some kind of family emergency. But don't worry, boss. I'm holding down the fort."

"Good to know. Hey, don't tell her I called. She's got enough on her plate and I don't want her to worry that her job is in jeopardy when it's not."

"I'm a vault, dude."

Nick hung up. "She left right after us."

"So that could be her." If she'd dressed like an older woman to hide her identity from anyone at that festival, and especially Zoe, then it was possible this woman was Candy and the woman who distracted him with the spilled purse was in cahoots with her.

Stehekin was a small community. But it wouldn't have been difficult to go into Seattle on her day off and collect the items she needed to disguise herself. YouTube makeup tutorials would make it super easy.

"Yeah. I mean…it could. But if it is Candy, then why hasn't Pepper alerted at the stables or in the conference room? Do you think she's alerting on the woman who distracted me? That can't be right, either. She wasn't the one who took Zoe."

He made valid points. But Pepper was never wrong. She'd smelled the same scent she'd been tracking the day Zoe disappeared and the same scent from the woods. It would be difficult for someone to mess with her sniffer. Not impossible. But pretty close. "Let's head in that direction. Easy and slow. Don't want to spook either of them."

But the older-looking woman who had on big sunglasses and a big hat walked away toward the falls. Pepper stayed on her. "You get the woman from the park. I'll stay with Pepper." Ruby kept going and followed the woman, holding the Lab back so as not to tip her off.

The crowd thickened as the shuttle bus approached. She and Pepper worked through the crowd, but then the bus left and Pepper lost her scent. She was either on the bus, or she'd slipped off behind the falls, with the massive amount of water acting as a barrier.

Ruby guided Pepper closer to the backside of the falls, hoping she'd regain the scent. As they went behind the rocks, the atmosphere grew eerie, ominous. Pepper maneuvered up the wet rocks and toward the waterfall, an area that was not part of the hiking trails. "Slow down, girl." Ruby was a good hiker and climber, but slow and steady won the race. Why had the woman come this way? She must have been familiar with the terrain up here. As Candy would be.

But Candy wasn't alerted on at the stables or in the house that morning Ruby met her. Why? Something didn't add up.

The sound of the rushing water grew louder, drowning out Ruby's voice as she called Pepper to slow again. Flecks of water bouncing off the boulders dotted her face and arms, and the temperature had cooled dramatically.

Pepper stopped, her nose low to the ground, then she sniffed the air. The temperature drop and lush vegetation, mixed with the water washing over rocks, had shifted and eroded the scent. It was possible the woman knew it, too. Which meant she was either familiar with dogs, or she knew she was being tracked and had done some googling on tracking dogs and what might mess with their scent detection.

Ruby sighed and rubbed the back of her neck. Maybe Nick had been more successful than her. As she turned to head down the rough terrain, a shadow bolted for her. She raised her hands to defend the quick lunge, but the attacker shoved her, knocking her off balance.

Pepper barked and growled. Ruby dropped the leash to keep from dragging her down the wet, slippery rocks. A jarring pain hit her ribs and she cried out as she stretched out for a rock to halt her fall.

But she missed.

"Nick!" she hollered, panic clogging her lungs. The waterfall was too loud. Too strong. He'd never hear her or get to her in time.

She tumbled over the embankment, free-falling into the raging currents and deadly waters.

Nick cornered the woman who had seen him. She'd tried to briskly walk away, but he'd intercepted her near the falls. "I haven't had a phone call from you. Your son change his mind?"

"Oh. Um…yeah." The woman shifted and darted her glance in the direction the other woman had hurried away.

"Cut it out. I know you set me up. Who was that woman you were with and what exactly did she tell you?" Nick asked.

"I have no idea what you're talking about."

"No, you do, and my daughter was kidnapped. You're an accomplice, which means you're going away for a long time."

The woman's eyes grew wide and tears filled them.

"I didn't know what was happening. She paid me two hundred dollars just to ask you that. She said you told her that you weren't taking new clients and she felt you were giving her the runaround because her son had some disabilities. She said if I asked and pointed to a little boy who was well and healthy, and you said no, then fine. But if you said yes, then she'd know you were being discriminatory and she was going to take action. Which I told her she should."

"That's the furthest from the truth. I would never."

"I didn't know," she insisted. "I thought I was helping a mom in need. And I could use the money. I'm backpacking across the Pacific Northwest before I start a new job in California. But when I read the news online that the little girl—your little girl—had been kidnapped, I put two and two together. I had no way to contact her but then today I saw her at the falls. I gave her the money back. I didn't want that money."

Nick's first thought was it was coincidental that she saw her at the falls, but the Rainbow Falls Loop and tour were very popular. "What's your name? Why didn't you call the authorities when you saw it?"

She shoved back her dark hair from her face. "I was scared. I didn't want to get in trouble. And I saw on the news that the girl made it home and was safe. I figured there was no point."

No point? He bit his tongue as a commotion stirred. A crowd was gathering, and a woman screamed.

"What's your name?"

"Lola Montana."

Nick made a face, then glanced toward the falls again. She held up her license. "Honest."

He took a photo with his cell phone. "I will find you if you leave this spot. You understand?"

"Yes, sir."

"Stay put." He rushed through the crowd to see a woman tumbling over the cliff into the current. "Ruby!" His heart slammed into his ribs and he made his way to the edge of the crowd, then slid and stumbled his way down to the bank, hoping to get a grasp. "Ruby! Can you hear me?"

She bobbed like a rag doll in the water. She was headed right for a huge boulder. He prayed and searched for anything that he might use to help her. A branch. Anything.

Ruby hit the rock and her head flung forward, then she went under.

Time froze. The world slanted.

His world.

She didn't resurface.

He didn't think. Didn't plan. He tossed his phone on the ground and dove off the side of the embankment, about six feet into the icy waters that nearly took his breath away. The current was powerful, pulling him down, but he fought and surfaced, searching for Ruby. He thought he saw the top of her head barreling toward another set of rocks. He willed himself to push through the current, to stay above water and get to her.

His shoulder slammed into an underwater rock and he felt a pop, then unbearable pain that stole his breath. He'd dislocated his shoulder. This had happened before. In the army. He now only had one arm, and the river was a force to be reckoned with.

But Ruby needed him.

And he needed Ruby.

Deep within, he felt bravado and raw power rise up.

He forged ahead. Ruby sank again and he dove beneath the surface, swimming, methodically searching until he found her. He encircled her waist and brought them up, holding her above the water, with him on his back, floating. He had no other choice. His good arm held her. He had no left arm with his shoulder dislocated.

But he needed to steer them out of harm's way and to the edge of the bank. He kicked, using all his muscle strength. Water sloshed over their faces, blurring his vision. Ruby was knocked out cold, a trickle of blood running down her temple. It didn't look terrible, but she'd hit her head enough to be rendered unconscious. Most likely had a concussion.

Nick was strong, but he wasn't stupid enough to believe he could keep this up much longer. The current was exhausting him. Every breath, every kick, was a fight and he was wearing down fast.

He blinked the water from his eyes and spotted a shadow in the water.

He blinked again.

Pepper! Pepper had jumped in after her handler and was making her way through the currents to them. The water covered her head, but she kept afloat, her nose upward as she moved those made-for-swimming paws under the surface until she met them.

"Hey, girl. Help us. Help Ruby, girl," he said and swallowed a rush of water, which brought on a coughing fit and burned his lungs. Pepper's mouth clamped onto his shirt collar and she began pulling them toward the bank.

He kicked and tried his best to aid the dog until finally they reached the opposite side of the embankment. Once he felt land on his feet, he hauled Ruby onto dry ground, then hugged that brave sweet Lab. "You're a good girl, Pep." He'd have never made it without her.

Nick checked Ruby's pulse. Strong. Good. He examined her head and felt a goose egg, then studied the cut on her forehead. Didn't need stitches. "Ruby," he said and lightly patted her cheek. "Hey, Ruby. Can you hear me?"

Her eyes fluttered and he moved away the hair matted to her cheeks. She moaned.

"It's okay. You're safe." He caressed her jawline and then her eyes opened. "Ruby? Can you hear me?"

"Yes," she said weakly.

"What day is it today?"

"Friday."

Good. "What state are you in?"

"A really bad one." She smirked and he laughed.

"I meant—"

"Washington State. I know what you meant." She struggled to sit up. Nick noticed tourists with cell phones across the river. "I think we're gonna break the internet today. Once they find a place to upload those pictures and videos. What happened?"

"I was pushed. By the woman who looked like Candy. Did you get to talk to the woman who distracted you in the park?"

"I did. But that can wait."

She sat up and groaned. "You jumped in to rescue me?"

"Then Pepper jumped in to rescue us both." He winced at the pain. "Hold tight." He got up and walked to the tree. "Don't watch."

"Watch what?" she mumbled and held her hand.

Nick positioned himself, then slammed his shoulder against the tree, feeling it relocate into position as he let out a scream at the stabbing pain. When it was nothing but a throb, he let out a breath and stumbled back over to Ruby, who was loving on Pepper and thanking her for saving them. The dog returned the kisses and Nick had never wished to be a dog more.

He gently grabbed her arm as she stood on wobbly legs. "You dizzy?"

"No. Just have a headache and I'd like to get out of here. Tend to my head. I'm bleeding."

Nick helped her maneuver through the forest until they were back at the trail and to where Lola Montana was still standing, her mouth hanging open. He mused that after seeing him dive off a cliff into raging water to save Ruby, she believed he'd come track her down, too.

"Come with us," he said and the woman followed obediently.

Nick tended to Ruby's wound with the first-aid kit he kept in the saddle bag. Once she was fixed up and had a couple of over-the-counter pain relievers, she turned her attention to Lola.

She repeated the same story to Ruby, and Nick believed her. Ruby gave him a look that said she did, too. And because of that, they let her go, but made sure they had her contact number and address. There wasn't much more she could do. She'd been duped.

But by Candy or someone else?

TWELVE

Ruby sat on the living-room couch, her head throbbing and her throat scratchy and raw from swallowing river water. The horse ride back had been bumpy but she'd been a trouper. She was about to call her mama. After all the cell-phone recordings and the park agents coming out, she had a feeling her mother would get wind. She paid close attention to the news in the parks now that Ruby had moved. Ruby used Nick's landline.

Mama answered on the first ring. "Well, I was wondering when you were gonna call and let me know you were alive. I saw the news. The photos online scared me half to death and the only thing that kept me from getting on a plane was that you were all right and safe. Saw Pepper and some horse guy rescued you. A man you been working a case with. His daughter went missing? What is going on down in that park, girlie?"

Ruby grinned at the worry in Mama's voice and the love that laced her words, even the scolding. She explained what she could about the case, Nick and Zoe.

"He dislocated his shoulder and still rescued you? Ruby, he's a keeper." She chuckled. "And his little girl sounds adorable."

"I'm not in the market for a man, Mama, and Zoe *is* adorable. So sweet." She propped up her feet and leaned her head back on the couch, closing her eyes.

"Is it because of Eli and that big dope before him? Not all men are gonna hurt you, honey."

"Yeah, well so far that's all they've done and I'm beginning to think it's not the men I choose, but me. I'm like a gravitational pull to losers, cheaters and liars. And now maybe even a murderer at worst, a scumbag at best. I don't know." Deep inside she believed that Nick was nothing but what he appeared to be. Good. Kind. Noble. Respectable. But she thought all those things from the other men she'd dated, too. "I've known him a week. We're still at the superficial stage."

"Are you being superficial?"

"No, ma'am."

"Then what makes you think he is?" Mama asked with sass in her tone. The question was not rhetorical.

"I don't know. I've just found that when something seems too good to be true, it typically is. It took decades for you to find Ray, Mama. I watched the pain—"

"I'm gonna stop you right there, missy. You and I are not the same, and you can't borrow my pain or my faith. You need to trust God and have the faith to believe that He has someone out there for you. This ain't no monkey see, monkey do, honey. And I'm gonna tell you something else you don't want to hear. You listening?"

As if Mama would allow anything less. "Yes, ma'am."

"You gotta stop blaming your daddy for your troubles, too. He walked out. Truth. He hasn't been good for us. Truth. But that doesn't mean you can't be everything you're supposed to be in Christ. Even if you had a daddy who stuck around and hung the moon, he wouldn't and couldn't take the place of your Heavenly Father. He would fall short every time. The best of daddies do. You been letting him dictate how you feel about yourself, your worth, your value. And it's affected your choices in men. Time to stop. Time to accept the fact and move forward. Stop wishing for things that didn't happen. Trust God to be enough. To lead you on. To make you whole and to fill you so full of His love—it's enough. It's more than enough."

Ruby's eyes stung and she wiped the tears that slipped under her lashes. "I know it is. But I'm struggling to believe it. To make the truth stick. How do you make the truth stick?"

"You glue it by faith to your heart. When you're doubtin', you say out loud the truth. 'I know my Father loves me. He never leaves me or forsakes me. He has a purpose for my life.' You speak that truth over yourself and let your faith cement it to your soul, baby girl. I had to do that every day working two jobs. I do it now just because I like the way the glue sticks." She chuckled again.

"I love you, Mama," she whispered.

"I love you, too. Stop getting pushed off cliffs. I'm old and my knees are bone on bone. You keep me on them too much lately."

She heard the humor in her voice. "Yes, ma'am. Give Ray my best."

"Open your heart up to love. When it's time, God will awaken it. Love you, baby."

"Love you." She opened her eyes and thought she saw a figure slip into the hall. She hung up and breathed a heavy sigh, then eased off the couch and down the hall. Nick was slipping into his home office. Had he overhead the conversation? Heard her say he might be superficial? He'd saved her life.

She entered the office. He'd changed, too. Naturally faded jeans and a fitted black T-shirt with the Cascades Stables logo in the middle. His hair was mussed; he stood by the window, looking out toward the stables. They'd been home for over an hour and it was nearing dinnertime. Zoe had taken a late nap.

"Hey."

"Hey," he said softly, his jaw working. Yep. He'd overheard.

"No news on Aaron Millsap. But they're looking for him. His name is on the manifest for the ferry two days before the kidnapping. There was a name below his. A woman's. We have no idea if she was with him, but we're running it."

"Good." His tone was tight.

She rounded the desk and stood behind him. She laid a hand on his shoulder. "What you heard. It's me, not you, Nick."

He gave a hard laugh. "The it's-not-you-it's-me speech. Nice." He turned, looming over her, his eyes intense and focused on hers. "I understand that you're hesitant to get into a relationship. I'm part of your case. I get that you've been hurt in the past by other men. But you can't lump me into the loser or superficial card. What you see is what you get. If you don't want what you see, then I get that, too, but you can't project those other men, or your father," he said in a hushed tone, "on me. That's not fair."

He was right. One hundred percent. "You're right. I know you're not putting on your best face only to change later. I know it here." She laid her hand on her heart. "But here—" she touched her temple "—here is where it gets murky and that's on me."

He cupped her cheek. "I would never hurt you, Ruby.

Not intentionally. I can't say never because I'm human. And you can't say you wouldn't hurt me. I haven't dated but once since Penelope. Haven't really wanted to. Until now. You think I'm not scared?"

She laid her hand on his, loving the feel of his fingers on her skin. The gesture gave her a measure of safety and comfort. "I don't know."

"Well, I am. I'm scared of how I feel about you. So fast. When I saw you free-falling, my heart pressed Pause and I was terrified."

She held his gaze.

"Not just scared someone was falling into the water and might drown, but terrified because it was you. You, Ruby. I didn't even think. I just jumped. And I'd do it again. I'd dislocate every single joint."

She believed him, but even so, the fear to say what she wanted was stuck. "Nick," she breathed and the rest of her sentence died on his lips as they met hers, softly and gently. The kiss was careful and slow until she wrapped her arms around neck, her fingers sliding into the hair at the nape of his neck.

She felt the strength, the honor, the truth in his sweet exploration. He led with skill and a sweetness she'd never felt before. His arms encircled her, resting his hands on her back as he pulled her closer to him and opened up more intimacy in their kiss, revealing his vulnerability. She returned it, unable not to. Because she did care about this man. So much.

But even caught up in a kiss that she could only describe as perfection, fear still pushed along the current, reminding her that she'd fallen headlong before.

Slowly and reluctantly, Nick ended their moment and kissed her forehead. "I'm not sorry for doing that."

Neither was she.

"But I know the timing is terrible on both our parts because Zoe is my number one priority right now. I can't ever be distracted again. So I'm sorry because here I am doing what I said I wouldn't do."

She understood. "I don't want to be a distraction."

"I didn't mean you were just a—"

"I know what you meant. And I've been through a lot. I need space and time to deal and figure out a lot of things about myself." Though she'd loved sharing a space with him if only for a few glorious moments.

"I understand, too." He let his hands slide from her back and stepped away, already respecting her need for space. "So let's talk the case. Because Candy isn't answering my calls and her husband, Garrett, said she'd called him and said her mom was sick and she was going to Seattle to see about her. Garrett confirmed that Candy's mom had cancer, so maybe it was true. Maybe not."

Did that mean Garrett might be in on this whole kidnapping plan, too? Or was Candy deceiving her own husband? And why? "If Candy is in desperate need of money then it's possible she's been approached by Aaron Millsap. The question is how would he get funds to pay her?" Ruby asked.

Nick shrugged. "I don't know. Could be from anywhere. We need to find him. And Candy. And we need to get Zoe out of here."

"That much we can do. Jackson has a safe house outside the park. We're likely being watched so we'll have to be careful. We can't tell anyone Zoe is leaving. No one. Only my team and you. That's it."

"When?"

"We'll move her before first light. You'll have a reason to be up and out—a sunrise tour led by you, so put a bug in your employees' ears so they believe it. We'll figure the rest out. I'll be out at the cabin office working."

Inside the cabin, Brandie sat with a concerned expression on her face. Her loose ponytail had lost some dark strands and they hung around her face.

"Hey. What's going on?" Ruby asked.

"Something happened today."

"Okay." She sat across from her. "Spill the tea, girl."

Brandie tucked a stray hair behind her ear. "Earlier, when I was out in the park with Dylan this morning—"

"Ah. I wondered what might progressing between the two of you, but haven't had a chance to ask."

Brandie's cheeks reddened. "No, not us. Why would you think that?"

Because she wasn't blind to see they were getting along well. Very well. "Why indeed?" She slipped off her roller brush and ran it down Brandie's leg. "I'm buying you one of these for yourself."

She smiled but it was distressed.

"Okay, so if it's not about you and Dylan, then what?"

"When we were out near Lake Chelan, I had a weird memory. It was blurry and in pieces, but I remember being there as a kid. As you all know, I've had these fuzzy memories from the start. I thought from the travel brochures I found in my parents' attic maybe I had been there very young. But with the way they always moved us around and the weird feeling that I didn't belong…well, I don't think for sure that the memory is about a vacation they took me on when I was a preschooler."

"That's where Lizzie Rossi went missing." Her stomach dipped.

"Exactly my point. So I did something else." She bit

her bottom lip and guilt sprang into her eyes. "Once we got back. Please don't be mad at me or kick me out of the candidates' program."

Ruby's heart ached for Brandie. She had no idea who she really might be. At least Ruby knew who her parents were. "Okay."

"I took a to-go coffee cup Nick used that he'd thrown in the trash. I sent it off to a private lab for DNA and asked a friend to put a rush on it. I need to know if that memory is really about Lake Chelan. I need concrete information."

"I see."

"I didn't want to ask Nick for DNA because I don't want to give him false hope. I don't want to have false hope. Trash is public property and not stealing. And if it's not a match, then maybe my memory is faulty, or it was a vacation, or has to do with someone or something else."

"Well, you didn't do anything illegal. You took trash and you are using a private lab with your own money. Still, I hate keeping this from Nick. It feels kinda wrong."

"Because of how you feel about him?" She smirked. "I can read body language, too."

"No." Maybe.

"Can we just not tell him? He's a nice guy and I would feel terrible if we smashed his hopes."

This put Ruby in a seriously tough predicament. She'd just kissed a man who professed he was honest because she hadn't believed him to be. Now, she was keeping a secret. One that might change his whole world, but she couldn't tip him off. And that felt dishonest.

"I won't say anything. I understand what you did and why."

"I catch him looking at me sometimes."

Ruby's gut twisted. "Like how?"

Brandie grinned. "Not romantically. Ew. He might be my brother. Like he's trying to figure out if he knows me from somewhere. Maybe it's because his sister and I both have dark hair and eyes and I am a close age. That's messing me up."

"Why? If your parents took you, you don't think they could have purchased fake papers and birth certificate? You're a cop. You know these things happen."

Brandie rubbed her temples. "Time will tell, I guess. In the meantime, I got a call from the babysitter, Hailey Alan. Apparently, she reached out to the ex-husband like she does sometimes, and he told her we were interested in talking to her."

"What else did she have to say?"

"That Nick and Lizzie had an aunt who adored Lizzie and doted on her. She took her on trips and for outings but never took Nick. Apparently she preferred docile little girls than 'wild' boys. Anyway, Mrs. Rossi had an argument with her sister, and the aunt stopped coming around."

Whoa. "Nick never mentioned it."

"He wouldn't. He didn't know. I called to verify it with Nick's parents and they admitted it was true, but never suspected her. They really had no reason to back then. But Nick's mom hasn't seen her sister but twice in guess how many years?"

"Twenty-five."

Well, this changed things.

It was almost 4:00 a.m. and Nick had barely slept last night after Ruby had told him about his aunt Kelly. She'd been around when he was little and he'd adored her, but then after Lizzie went missing everything changed. He'd assumed Aunt Kelly never coming around was part of that. He never questioned or asked about her at first. Then he'd asked why she never visited. Mom had called Kelly a free spirit who liked to travel and wasn't one to take much responsibility or think too much of others. They'd had an argument and Kelly had gone off on one of her adventures.

Kelly had often talked of traveling the world with friends, so when she'd left, they assumed she'd finally had. They'd heard from her a few times by phone over the years, but that was it. They never suspected Aunt Kelly of abducting Lizzie. Nick wasn't sure she had, either.

But he had no way to get in touch with her. Ruby had her team tech analyst tracking her down. After hanging up with his parents, he'd busied himself cooking a light dinner for himself, Ruby and Zoe. Jacqueline had taken some time off before it was time to go to the safe house.

They'd eaten quietly, except for Zoe, who was very excited to go on a trip with Jacqueline and her dog, Jesse. Nick thanked God that Zoe was taking this well and was happy, and not terrified.

Like he was.

He'd packed her up and put her items in a backpack he'd use for hiking. She and Ruby had watched the fish movie again and he'd noticed Ruby's extra cuddles with his baby girl. It seemed so natural and right.

Now it wasn't even dawn and he was brewing a pot of coffee, then going out to the stables alone to set up the day like he'd done yesterday, establishing a new routine. That gave him reason to be up before the crack of dawn, so he could see his baby girl off without tipping off the kidnapper if they were watching.

Ruby entered the kitchen in sweats and a T-shirt. Sleepy-eyed but beautiful to him. "You ready?"

"No. But I understand this is what needs done. It's the anniversary of my sister's disappearance today. My daughter is leaving me to a place I can't even know. I have to trust people I'm only familiar with and hope nothing goes sideways. Is anyone ready for that?"

She poured a cup of coffee. "No. Zoe will be safe. Plus, another one of our team members will be there with her suspect-apprehension K-9. Danica is great and Jackson you've met. You know Jacqueline is on her game. And we'll figure out who is behind this and where Aaron Millsap is hiding out as well, as why Jeremy Benedict was found dead near your home."

"And what if nothing happens tonight? How long does Zoe stay in a safe house? How long do we hide the fact that she's not here? How long do you stay?" He knew she had to leave. She had a job to do and he was keeping focused on his daughter, but the thought of never seeing her again sent a crack to his chest.

He didn't want that. Their kiss had meant something. More than he wanted to admit. And from the way she'd kissed him back, it had meant more to her, too.

But the thought she'd revealed to her mom, that he'd overheard, had crushed him. Ruby had been hurt many times and one was most recent. He had to put that into perspective and not take it personally, but it felt personal. He rubbed his still-sore shoulder.

"I know she'll be okay. I'm trusting God to take care of her. It's just, even so…we never know. I trusted Penelope with God, too, and she died." He'd come to terms with God's sovereignty. Sometimes He intervened, and sometimes not. Those reasons were beyond Nick's pay grade. He only needed to trust God regardless. To remember He was good, anyway. Faithful, anyway. He'd felt God's closeness and comfort throughout the loss and grief. Though some days he'd been spitting mad at God. Some days, just sad and confused.

Finally, he'd come to terms with it and made peace. Grieved but knew one day he would see Penelope again. She was with Him.

Ruby took his hand and squeezed. "Not that it brings you any more comfort, but I'll be with you every step of the way. I'm not leaving until we find who did this and if it ends up meaning on my own time, then so be it. We're in this now, together."

Actually, that brought a lot of comfort to Nick. "That means more than you know. You've been nothing but honest with me and I appreciate it."

She smiled then it faltered, and he wondered what thought had turned the mood around so quickly. Had she not been open and honest about something?

"Let's get going. Jackson and Danica will meet us at the floatplane at the dock before sunrise. It's safer for Dylan to fly them out of Stehekin. Too many eyes on the ferry. Jacqueline will be with Zoe and keep a medical eye on her."

"But Goldie won't be with her." Goldie had to stay behind or it wouldn't work. The kidnapper would know Zoe wasn't here. The dog went everywhere with her. But not having Goldie meant no one would know a seizure was coming. Nick's stomach was in knots.

Ruby took his hands again and prayed for Zoe's safety and Nick's peace. Her prayer meant the world to him.

Time to play hide-and-seek with Zoe. Because they didn't know who was watching, they were going to have to get her out without being seen. Which meant walking out wasn't happening.

He awoke her and she hugged him with sleepy eyes. "You ready to go on your big adventure on a plane with Officer Jacqueline today?"

Suddenly, her grogginess was gone and replaced with excitement. "Yes. But I'll miss Goldie and you and Officer Ruby."

"I know. We'll miss you, too. But we'll be here when you get back. And you can play with Taz and some other dogs, too. And Ridge. You like Ridge." She loved Dylan's Saint Bernard.

"Okay, Daddy."

Nick heated up a couple of the frozen pancakes and got her dressed. Ruby came downstairs with one rolling suitcase and Jacqueline followed with another. It would appear that only Jacqueline would be leaving.

When had it come to this? Hiding his child away so she wouldn't be kidnapped? The fear and pain shot through him, but he returned it with prayer for peace and that this would go according to plan with no hitches and no seizures.

"Daddy is going to count and we're going to hide. Ready? Just like we practiced last night after we watched the movie," Ruby whispered.

Nick turned his head, tears burning the back of his eyes as he knew what was happening. He heard the huge suitcase unzip and his daughter giggle as she put her tiny frame inside, then he heard it zip again, but not all the way.

"Be real quiet okay. We're gonna hide in the car like last time and then remember when I unzipped you?"

"Yep. I'm gonna be real quiet. Daddy won't find me."

No. He wouldn't. Because it was in everyone's best interest that he didn't know where the safe house was. *Lord, help me though this.*

It would be like Jacqueline was leaving with her luggage. No child. No dog. She would take the vehicle she brought for Ruby back with her and leave Ruby without one again. Just like it began. They'd drive to the dock in Nick's truck later to see Jacqueline off in a a floatplane and then drive to a safe house from the landing. The stack of papers Nick had to sign last night were beyond detailed.

Jacqueline headed for the door and paused long enough to whisper everything would be okay. Jackson would call Ruby later when they were settled. But it would be about four to five hours. That seemed like eternity to Nick.

Once they left and were backing from the drive, Nick swallowed hard. "I should get the horses ready for the ride."

"Are you sure you want me to come with?"

"It wouldn't make sense if you didn't. Zoe will want to tell you 'bye one last time. You've been with us since it started and us not being together won't look right." He swallowed at those last words. Them not being together didn't seem right. But things were wonky. "But I would like to get the horses together myself. I need some time alone, if you don't mind. Need to wrap my head around the fact that I won't be around my daughter for the first time since she's been born."

"I won't dare say I understand what you're feeling because I don't. I can't. But I do know what it's like to feel loss, helpless and vulnerable. I'm so sorry this is happening and I hope we find who is doing this soon. Everything is pointing to Candy."

He knew that but it still hurt. He'd opened up his life and home to her. He knew between fertility treatments and the costs to prepare and adopt that it was superexpensive, but to allow someone like Aaron Millsap to bribe her with cash to hurt him and take Zoe. Unless Aaron lied to her. Or something else entirely was going on. They had today to figure it out. And he would. Because he couldn't handle a day without Zoe, let alone possibly a week. He refused to be apart any longer than that.

"I know. Maybe today we'll get answers."

"I hope so. Go on out."

"I'll saddle Maple for you. She liked you."

Ruby grinned. "I liked her, too."

"You sure you're up to getting back on a horse?"

"The ride had been good. It wasn't Maple that messed up the day. It was getting pushed off the cliffs. I actually was enjoying myself up until then. Go on. Get saddled up."

"Yes, ma'am." He winked and headed toward the stables.

Inside, he went into Candy's office and rifled through the papers on her desk. Her calendar caught his eye. An hour was blocked out three weeks ago with the initials *JB* in red. Then it was written again a little over a week ago. JB.

Just before Jeremy died. Could Candy have been meeting with Jeremy Benedict? And if so, had he been in on this, too?

THIRTEEN

Ruby had come to care deeply for Zoe. She didn't realize how much it would hurt to see her leave until right now, as the little dark-haired girl hugged her tight and buried her little face into Ruby's neck.

"Ruby, I don't wike you anymore."

Her heart pinched.

"I wuv you," she whispered in her ear.

Her insides turned to jelly and she hung on to Zoe, not wanting to let her go. She'd grown attached, and would miss their evening playtime and snuggles. "I love you, too, sweet Zoe. You're going to have such a big time."

Her big blue eyes filled with moisture. "Okay."

"You're so brave." She handed her the Peter Rabbit book and *The Velveteen Rabbit*. "Officer Jacqueline will read you these until I can again. You think of me when she does, okay?"

She clutched the little books and nodded. She was putting on such a brave front. Ruby framed her chubby little face and kissed her forehead. "It won't be long."

She nodded again, her bottom lip quivering.

Nick kneeled and Zoe ran into his arms, nearly throwing him off balance, and Ruby wiped the moisture from her eyes as Nick said his final goodbye to Zoe. They'd ridden out on a secluded trail and had been careful not to be followed. Ruby had remained quiet, letting Nick process, think and probably pray. She loved that he was a man of faith, strong faith.

Maybe that had been part of Ruby's problems before. She'd never made faith a priority in the men she dated. The fact that they went to church was enough for her. Grandmama always said God expected women to marry godly men. Ruby had settled on companionship. She'd learned her lesson, though, this time.

Zoe hugged Nick tight, but it was Nick who hung on longer, not wanting to let his baby girl go. Jacqueline had reassured him multiple times that Zoe would be safe, protected and cared for. It would be the time of her life. Ruby trusted in that. Believed wholeheartedly that Zoe was in the best of care.

But that didn't make it any easier on Nick, and it broke Ruby's heart to see him wiping his eyes, his throat bobbing and his jaw twitching. Oh, to have someone love her like Nick loved Zoe. He backed away, Zoe waving through the small window. Dylan gave them the thumbs-up and the engine roared. Ruby stepped up and took Nick's hand to offer him moral support.

He squeezed it and waved at Zoe with the other hand, then the plane skimmed down Lake Chelan and lifted into the predawn sky. They watched in silence until they could no longer see the plane. Nick sniffed and wiped moisture from his eyes.

"You need a hug?" she asked.

Nick embraced her, holding tight, as if her hold truly gave him comfort. That was a new feeling as well. She'd always found that she needed the hugs, but no one she'd dated had ever looked or needed emotional support from her.

"It's going to be okay," she whispered against his chest. They stood on the dock hugging as the sun peeked over the trees and brushed the sky with pink and purple hues. But she couldn't stay like this. She had a job to do. And she was keeping a secret. That Brandie had taken a cup he'd thrown in the trash because she thought she might be Nick's sister. She needed to break the connection and contact between herself and Nick.

"I guess it's just that today is the day Lizzie left my life and this park and now I've had to watch Zoe leave me on the same day. I'd love to tell you I'm tough as steel and can handle anything, but the truth is, I'm just a man, Ruby. I'm made of flesh and blood and I'm struggling today." He clung tighter and she relished his honesty and vulnerability.

Yet, she wasn't being honest with him, though it was to protect him if nothing came of Brandie's search. Still, it felt wrong.

"No one expects you to be a hero, Nick. It's okay to be hanging by a thread as long as you know that you're not going to snap and break. God has you in the palm of His hand, even if it doesn't feel like that." How many times had Grandmama told her that? Too many to count.

"I know," he whispered. "Even in all this mess, I feel His presence in my life. Like He's doing something I can't see. I just wish it didn't involve my daughter. I wish it wasn't something that was going to be born out of pain."

"My mama says everything truly precious is born of pain. I was worth the forty-eight hours of pain she endured. That holding me made every tear, all the sweat, all the groans, worth it. But the pain seems so overwhelming at the time, there's no way to get past it to see what might be on the way that brings new hope and new life."

"Your mom sounds amazing. I'd love to meet her someday."

At that comment, she did break the hold. "She'd like you, no doubt." Ruby patted Pepper's head. "Now, let's get to work and set up a game plan for tonight." There was a real possibility that the kidnapper would make a move at some point today or tonight.

Back at the house, they kept the blinds closed, minus the ones that were still boarded and awaiting custom windows next week. Goldie was still around so if anyone was watching they'd assume Zoe was here. She never left her dog.

After a quick breakfast of eggs and toast, Ruby and Nick set out. By eight, Candy called Nick and said she'd come down with the flu and wouldn't be in the rest of the week. Nick wasn't buying it, and neither was Ruby.

"Do we go over there and confront her or let the day play out and see what happens?" Nick asked.

Ruby had wondered that herself. "Let me confer with our chief. This could go either way." She left the house and walked out to the office/cabin. Brandie was inside on her computer. "How many days off do you have left?"

"Just two. The precinct has been so good to let me off when needed. I have the best captain." She grinned. "I've narrowed down five abductions around the time of Lizzie Rossi's that could be me. All around the parks here in Washington. But after that memory at Lake Chelan... I don't know. Why would my parents have taken me? I just don't understand their motives. They were paranoid and always a little strict and we moved often, but they weren't bad people. They never hurt me or mistreated me, or were cruel. For most children abducted, we all know that isn't the case. Maybe I'm wrong. Maybe I'm imagining it."

"You're not. You found those papers that didn't add up and the brochures that made you think you might have been abducted from one of parks. Then you had that memory that matched the one you've been having before seeing the lake. I don't know why you were abducted…if you were."

"Why wouldn't God have prevented it?" Brandie asked. "Why allow me to be ripped from my real family?"

"These are questions above my pay grade, Brandie. But Joseph was ripped from his family for over thirty years. God used what was evil for good. He didn't prevent it. So maybe—maybe just look for and hope for the good." That sounded somewhat trite but it was all she had.

"I don't see God making me the prime minister of Egypt."

Ruby smirked. "Hey, you never know."

They chuckled the heaviness of the topic away. "On another note, Candy called in sick. I need to talk to the chief. See how he wants me to play this. I need advice."

"I feel like preventative care is best. If she's going to attempt another kidnapping. Thwart it. Don't let it play out. It could go sideways." Brandie pointed to herself. "I should know."

She was right. Preventing was better than picking up pieces when an abduction could be prevented. And maybe this could. She could surely avoid more heartache by not choosing the same types of men she'd chosen before. "Okay, then Nick and I are going over to Candy Reynolds's home. You keep watch over the house. If anything weird happens or looks odd, call me on the satellite phone."

"Will do."

Ruby paused and caught her eye. "And hang in there. God's got this." And He had Ruby, too. She needed to remember that and hang in there as well. She left the cabin and Nick stood outside with a backpack slung across his back.

"I figured we'd take the UTV. We can move faster and cover both rough terrain and roads if needed. That work for you?"

"Sounds good to me."

"Is Brandie okay?" he asked as they walked toward the utility shed where he kept it. "She seems off, and on occasion, I catch her staring at me."

Ruby's gut clenched. She had to tread lightly. She didn't want to lie to Nick, but she also couldn't reveal Brandie's confidence and give him the possibility of false hope and definitely not on this day. She hated keeping secrets. "Why do think she's staring at you?"

"I don't know. Funny thing, she said something the other day that I felt like I've heard before. But you told her it wasn't a saying."

"What's that?"

Nick adjusted his backpack. "She said, 'Princesses only wake up pretty if they get beauty sleep.' I know I've heard that. Maybe a movie. Zoe has so many princess movies and books. It could be either."

"It's possible."

"What's her story?"

"Brandie?" Ruby's gut twisted again. "She's a K-9 officer in a small town outside the park. She's twenty-seven."

"Oh." He paused outside the utility shed. "I can't help but look at young women who would be about the same age as Lizzie and have brown hair and eyes. I look at photos and I think would she look like that now? I'm losing my memories of her without the photos. I hate that, Ruby. So much."

Ruby's throat clogged. "I'm sorry. I wish it was different and that you didn't have to go through it each day."

"I know. It helps talking about it. For a long time I didn't. My wife, Penelope, didn't even know about it until we'd been dating almost a year and I took her home to meet my parents. I knew she'd see photos. It was just so hard."

"I get it."

"But it's not hard to share with you. And it feels good to talk about it." He opened the door and startled.

"What is it?" she asked and inched forward.

"Aaron Millsap."

Ruby peeked inside the utility shed and Aaron Millsap was lying in a heap, dried blood on his head.

Nick stood beside the shed as ISB agents and their crime-scene techs surveyed the area. One approached and he cocked his head. He looked familiar and then recognition dawned. "Zeke Moore?"

The man had filled out over the years and his hair was darker, but he still had the scowling dark eyes and pinched lips. Moore had been the baseball hero in high school and had played in the minor leagues but never went on to the pros. It was a mystery.

Agent Moore grinned. "Nick Rossi. How ya doing?" He shook Nick's hand. "Sorry we're seeing each other again under these circumstances." His gaze switched to Ruby, who had walked over. He spotted her name badge. "Agent Orton. Zeke Moore. I'm with the ISB. Your chief caught me up to speed before I flew in. Anything else I need to know to help you."

Their PNK9 team was already doing the crime-scene processing and Ruby was running point with the investigation, but the Investigative Services Branch would help take a load off, especially with the other cases the PNK9 team was dealing with.

Ruby filled him in, and Agent Moore rubbed the back of his neck. "I didn't see any drag marks."

"We think he may have been hiding out in the shed. We found boot prints last week. We're just not sure if Aaron's death is in connection with Jeremy Benedict's death. Originally, we thought maybe Aaron killed Jeremy, though we couldn't determine the motive, but if that was true then who killed Aaron? And why?" Ruby sighed. "Any help would be appreciated."

"You got it." He looked to Nick. "I need to get to work but let's catch up later. It's good seeing you and I'd like to hear what you've been up to. I only know you went into the military. CID."

"That's right. We'll catch up once we get whoever is behind all this." He shook his hand again.

"I want to visit Candy Reynolds's house now," Ruby said. The UTV was stuck in the shed, which was a crime scene. Techs had discovered an old shovel that had blood on it. It appeared to be the murder weapon, but they couldn't say for certain until the tests came back.

"We'll take the truck." Nick led Ruby to his vehicle and they headed down the road to Garrett and Candy Reynolds's house.

Nick took the lead and knocked on the door. No one answered. But Garrett's truck was in the driveway and they didn't have a garage or carport, so where was

Candy's car if she was sick with the flu? He rapped on the door again, louder and longer. Garrett opened the door, his eyes bloodshot and hair disheveled. It looked like he'd worn the same shirt for several days and his usual clean-shaven face was covered in a little more than scruff.

"Garrett."

"Hey," he said and offered them access to the house. "I guess you're here about Candy."

Nick exchanged a surprised look with Ruby. "Yeah. She here?"

"No. Things have been weird between us."

"Weird how?" Nick asked.

Garret rubbed his red eyes. "I thought at first her behavior was odd due to the last fertility treatment not working. Then I thought the evasiveness and shiftiness was from the financial stress of planning for an adoption." He walked to the coffeepot, poured a cup and held up the carafe as an invitation.

Neither accepted.

He sat at the table beside them. "The shady behavior progressed. Late-night phone calls. Skittish as a horse. I'd gotten a second job to help with the extra money to apply for adoption or whatever we needed to do to start a family. Things didn't change."

"And today? Where is she today?"

He looked at Nick. "Joe called and checked in on her since she had the flu. Imagine my surprise. I thought she'd left today and gone to work. She's not sick. I never dreamed she'd leave me…but what else could it be? Everything adds up to someone on the side."

Couldn't be Aaron Millsap, he was dead. Couldn't be Jeremy Benedict. He was dead, too. Unless… He glanced at Ruby and her stern expression revealed that she was thinking the same thing.

Somehow Candy must have gotten mixed up in Aaron Millsap's plan to exact revenge and may have enlisted Jeremy Benedict. They'd become friends while working together for him. Nick never suspected an affair, though. Either someone else was involved or the heat got hot and Candy killed Aaron and Jeremy. But why?

"You say her behavior had progressively gotten stranger? As in the past few months?" Ruby asked.

Garrett held his cup, steam rising. "Definitely more erratic and more secretive. I want a baby, too. So much. But Candy's been unhealthy about it. Obsessing. When I heard that Zoe had been taken… I'll be honest. I thought it might be Candy. She's been on some meds to help her with the anxiety and to sleep. But she stopped taking them a couple of months ago."

"Do you think she took Zoe?"

"No. I mean, the Candy I married never would have done a thing like that. But the Candy now…maybe."

It's possible she'd taken her the first time, then had second thoughts. But why leave her on the ledge? That was psychological torture for Nick, which made more sense for Aaron Millsap, who wanted revenge. It was the only reason for him to be here lurking and hiding illegally in unoccupied cabins.

They'd never know Aaron's motives, though. He was dead. But who put him in there? Nick had put a lock on the door after they'd discovered footprints inside. The only other people with a key would be Joe and Candy.

"When she told me she'd gotten a raise and I could quit my second job at the ferry, I thought maybe she wasn't stepping out on me—"

"She told you she got a raise?" Nick hadn't given Candy a raise since she became manager two years ago. "She said you wanted her home more. Is that true?"

"No. We did discuss her working less, or not at all after we had a baby, or adopted, but until then we were trying to work as much as possible to save. Why would she say that?"

"I never gave her a raise, Garrett. Why would she say *that*?"

Ruby tented her fingers on the table. "Did you notice an uptick in finances?"

"I honestly don't know. Candy's always been good with the money so she does our finances. I'll have to look." Nick rubbed his chin.

"How was the money deposited? Check or cash?" Nick asked.

Garrett shook his head. "I'll have to go get the passwords book. I don't even know it." He quietly left the kitchen.

"What do you think?" Nick asked.

Ruby pursed her lips. "I really don't know what to think. Pepper would have alerted on her if she was the scent in the woods and by the lake where Zoe was left. She didn't."

"Except think about it. You've only been around Candy a few times. At the house, and Pepper was sitting. If she circled and sat, would you have paid any attention?"

Ruby rubbed her chin. "Out in the field, yes. In the safety of your home with people you love and trust. Not so much. She was sitting next to me the whole time. And then the only other time we had contact was at the stable that day. Pepper was with Zoe, Jacqueline and Goldie in the house." Ruby rubbed her temples. "But Pepper should be able to scent her from the house to the stable. I mean, there are factors that make a scent easy to lose. The storm. Change in wind. It's unlikely but not out of the realm of possibility."

"Do you think she's unhinged enough to try to kidnap Zoe again if it's her?"

"I think it's worth setting up a sting to see. This makes more sense than her cheating on her husband. But if she does take Zoe, where would she go with her? She surely knows Garrett would have no part. And why kill you?"

Nick had no clue. This entire scenario was bum-fuzzling. "If she thought I'd come after her—which I would—eliminating me would be the only way to run with her. But I can't see her leaving Garrett."

"I read about a case where a woman kidnapped a child and killed her husband when he told her she had to turn herself in. She wanted the child so badly and was unstable enough to believe she had a well-thought-out plan. And there have been many other true-crime cases of the same type of thing. So…again, it's possible."

Garrett came back into the room. "I called the bank."

"And?" Nick asked.

"She deposited six sums of two thousand dollars over the past three months in cash. Twelve thousand total. But yesterday morning she withdrew all of it." He slumped in his chair. "She's left me."

Maybe. Even more importantly, where did she get that kind of money? And why?

FOURTEEN

Ruby concluded that Candy couldn't have gone far. They'd checked the floatplane and ferry manifests. Her name wasn't on there. Unless she'd gotten fake IDs, which was possible, too. Ruby never put anything past desperate people. She'd seen some of the most depraved things working in Mobile. People went to great lengths to hurt others and get what they wanted, whether it was power, fame, fortune or even revenge—especially revenge.

They'd had a quick lunch and canvassed the businesses and lodges, hoping someone had seen Candy or heard from her, but they didn't get a single lead. No one had seen her or Aaron Millsap for that matter. The day dragged on as they worked every angle they had. To thank Nick for his hospitality, Ruby had cooked Nick proper shrimp and grits, which he ate wholeheartedly and had thirds. Then they'd gone over every part of their investigation until the clock was about to strike 8:00 p.m.

She wasn't sure how to fit all the pieces into the puzzle. It was like they had a lot of middle pieces but no edges. The edge pieces needed to be placed first, to frame the picture within and right now, Ruby had no framework, only theories and ideas.

Candy didn't appear irrational or erratic from Ruby's observations. But she had been a bit cagey the past week and avoided them. Someone had paid her a great deal of money. Which meant she'd done something to earn that money. What? And why did it start three months ago? Could she have been paid to watch Nick and Zoe? To help Aaron Millsap get to Stehekin? Was she the girlfriend? Ruby had far more questions than answers at this point.

Now she sat at the Stehekin Lodge with her laptop and Brandie Weller, and joined the video call the chief had set up. One by one, her colleagues' faces popped on screen. They smiled and made a little small talk, but the stolen pups and Mara's vanishing weighed heavy on all their minds and was the reason for less banter and jokes.

"How's the case?" Jackson asked, his background a tropical island to hide his location at the safe house.

She briefed them and asked about Zoe. "She's doing great. Jacqueline is keeping her occupied and she's literally been taking horseback rides through the place, only instead of a horse, she's using Ridge. She calls him Pony-Ridge."

Ruby smiled. Nick would be happy to hear that. At the moment, he was at home. "Agent Zeke Moore with a lot of questions for Nick. They can't rule him out."

She'd hated that he was now a person of interest in this case. "Local rangers are looking for Candy Reynolds." But she'd lived in the Cascades her whole life, so finding her wouldn't be easy. She knew trails and places no one knew of and might have even had secret help getting out of the valley. For all Ruby knew, Candy could be anywhere. But if she was fixated on Zoe, she'd make one more play for her.

Tonight.

The chief popped on and greeted them. "Good to see all your faces. Let's get down to the nitty-gritty. We all have a lot on our plates. What's the next step for you, Ruby?"

"Well, it's the anniversary of Nick's sister's disappearance. I think the kidnapper might make a play tonight. The timing of the first abduction isn't a coincidence. This night means something to the abductor." She frowned.

"What is it?"

"We don't know but we have a trap set." She told them what they were going to do and everyone hoped it would work.

"Keep us posted. Brandie, how's the cold case coming?"

"I don't have any news as of yet. But we'll see." She didn't mention the cup with the DNA and Ruby sat quietly.

"Asher, you're up," Chief said.

"Tanner and I went to the Stark Lodge earlier to talk with Eli Ballard, Stacey Stark's business partner. He was super chill and told the same story he did at first. Nothing has changed. He hasn't deviated. It's not verbatim each time, which would make me suspicious, but it hasn't skewed and that makes me think he could be telling the truth. However…before we left, Layla's K-9 alerted at the basement again. Again, he says it's just family rifles. I wish we had probable cause to check. I don't trust this guy."

Ruby's stomach roiled.

"Sorry, Ruby," Tanner said.

"No. It's okay. He may not be trustworthy."

Willow Bates's dog had alerted at a basement door at one of the other Stark Lodges prior to this latest alert, and Eli had told them it was family hunting rifles. With no probable cause to search and him not being a suspect at the time, they let it go. But now with Layla's dog alerting at a different lodge and knowing what they did now concerning the photo of Mara and Asher's poor dad in the assisted-living home and Eli Ballard having been there, it might mean something more dangerous.

Layla spoke, "Bixby was pretty keyed up. I feel like it could be more than just a few family heirlooms." Layla was the rookie on the PNK9 team, only with them for two months. She was an all-American beauty with long blond hair and green eyes. Petite but strong. Ruby hadn't worked with her much, but she liked her.

"A keyed-up dog won't get us a warrant," Asher said. "One photo of my dad isn't enough, either. We can't say how many guns might even be down there. We're going to go back later when Eli's gone and see if we can get the night manager, Brad Sheffield, to oblige us and give us access to look around."

The guns and then the drugs. Now more possible guns. How deep was this? And could Eli have a reasonable explanation for being at the nursing home after a photo of the Gilmore siblings' father had surfaced, and had likely been used to blackmail Mara into silence? Ruby didn't want to believe that Eli was the real killer. But she couldn't deny that he could be.

Even if he hadn't become a person of interest, if he had absolutely nothing to do with the murders, Ruby would probably still be with him and falling deeper in love with a good man. But not a godly man.

It had taken coming here under horrific circumstances for her to see the contrast between good and godly. Nick was both. That fact, along with her talk with her mama, had opened her eyes to see truth. She wanted both. Good and godly.

Grandmama used to say that sometimes God took His people the long way around the mountain to teach them to trust and depend on Him. Ruby had definitely been going around the mountain.

"Any news on the bloodhound pups?" Jackson asked.

"We got the results from the receipt and drugs found in the ice caves. The same dog hair on the receipt and the brick of cocaine, and it was cocaine," Chief said, "were a match and the same hair matched the samples of our puppies, so they were there. The receipt is for a purchase from a food truck from the Salt Creek Recreation Area near Port Angeles and Olympic National Park."

This meant that the puppies had been in the cave and that whoever stole them was also connected to drug running. Between the puppies' case and Mara's situation, things were intense. Why would drug runners want the pups? Other than they would likely go for a lot of money. Still.

"That brings us to the next item of business," Chief said. "Asher and I will be heading to the Salt Creek Recreation Area and Olympic National Park undercover. These guys obviously came from there and likely went back. We're hoping to get some concrete information and it's best if we go in not looking, dressing or acting as PNK9 officers. We'll be leaving in three days."

"Do you need any assistance?" Owen, one of the candidates for the team, asked. He'd been working on the back end at headquarters with fellow candidate Veronica, and likely felt out of the loop. "I'm happy to lend a hand."

"Too many of us would be suspicious. But thanks,

Owen. I appreciate your team-player attitude." The chief nodded.

Ruby caught Parker roll his eyes and refrained from saying anything. For someone claiming innocence on trying to sabotage the other candidates, eye rolling wasn't exactly supporting that claim.

After a few moments of more business and then just some light conversation, which always brought the team closer, they ended the call. Ruby stood and stretched—her back ached and she was exhausted. "You want to come back to Nick's?"

"Actually, I'd like to stay here at the lodge. I want to stay on my laptop and run down a few things. Besides, I have over one hundred emails and I need to wade through them. Unless you think you need me tonight?"

If Candy was going to strike, tonight seemed prime. They were going to be ready for her. "No. Between Nick and I, we can handle it. We've got the upper hand." She hoped.

"Okay. Be careful."

"Will do." She gathered her belongings and led Pepper out of the Stehekin Lodge and into the cool night, the wind chilling her skin. She untied her windbreaker from around her waist and slipped into it. She and Brandie had brought Nick's UTV to the lodge, leaving him with his truck. Better that he should stay home. Anyone who had been stalking his habits knew he was home for good by six and spent time with Zoe. He was going to make sure and play enough with the dog to get her to bark, so anyone who might be lurking would hear and believe Zoe to be inside.

Nick was going to be so happy to hear Zoe was doing

well. She cranked the UTV but the engine wouldn't roll over.

She tried again. Two more times.

Nothing.

Goose bumps that had nothing to do with the weather prickled along her arms and the hairs on her neck stood on end. Something about this didn't feel right. Not that she knew what she was doing, but she popped the hood of the vehicle and stared at it. If anything was wrong, she'd never know. Mechanics wasn't her forte.

She pinched the bridge of her nose, then noticed the smell of gasoline. She rounded the vehicle and noticed the scent grow stronger. "This is your job, Pep." She chuckled and squatted, noticing that the grass was wet. She touched it and brought her fingers to her nose.

Gasoline.

She took out a tissue and wiped the ground to get the scent on it. She held it out to Pepper. "Track."

Pepper sniffed the air and began moving, then she lowered her nose to the ground, circled and sat a few feet away. Ruby once again squatted and saw the grass was wet. Her suspicions confirmed. Someone had siphoned the UTV's gas tank, spilling it and then sloshing it out.

"Track."

Pepper repeated the same thing. Sniff and alert, every few feet, until she reached the edge of the parking lot and lost the scent. Likely when the gas thief drove away. Why? Why steal her gas?

Because someone wanted her stranded, or at least slowed down.

Which meant whoever was behind this was on the move and wanted Ruby out of the picture.

Nick might be in danger.

No, he surely was in danger.

Nick had sat on Zoe's bed for over an hour with the blinds drawn, but the lamp on and the child-sized doll in the bed as a Zoe placeholder. But nothing was a placeholder for his little girl. The more he'd contemplated on the day and Candy's behavior, the more defeated he felt.

His phone rang and he answered. It was Zeke Moore from the ISB. "Hey, Zeke."

"Hey, man. I know it's really late but I wanted to touch base with you. So the lab called and we have two full sets of prints. There was also a partial print on the shovel, which is going to take longer to match."

"It could be my late wife's. That shovel has been around for ages."

"Maybe. But the other print besides yours that we did match is a Candy Reynolds. I checked and saw she works for you. Manager."

Nick's heart sank. "Yeah." Ruby had talked about not trusting her judgment. Nick was feeling as if he was in the same boat. How could he be so wrong about a person?

"We went to her house about an hour ago. Husband says you came by earlier. He filled me in on what you know. Hasn't heard from her and her phone is off so we can't ping it if she's out of the valley and where there is cell service."

"Anything new you do know?"

"Well, I decided to run with the abduction of your daughter and what's transpired since. Jeremy Benedict was camping. We've verified that. We searched his house and got a warrant for his laptop. Yeah. He has one."

"Probably used it where there was limited access."

"Probably. We found a resignation letter. The date was for next week, though. That would make a two-week notice from the day he was found dead."

Nick processed. He'd gone camping. Taken a few days off, maybe to get the time in that he wouldn't receive if he resigned, or to think about something. About quitting. He writes the note then shows up on Nick's property. "Do you think he was coming to ask for his job back and someone killed him?"

"I think it's plausible. He didn't drive and came through the woods which he was prone to do. You said he often walked to work. So maybe he's on his jaunt, thinking about asking you for his job back and sees something or someone he shouldn't and he's killed."

Nick massaged the back of his neck. "Or he was on to Candy. They knew each other pretty well. She might have killed him to silence him."

"That works, too." He laughed lightly. "Seriously, man, we could use more ISB agents. We only have about thirty and we could use a guy with your skills."

"And work with you? I don't know," he teased. "The truth is I know it requires a lot of travel and at a moment's notice. Zoe is only three."

"I hear ya. That makes sense. But between me, you and my boss… I'm leaving at the end of the month. Took a detective job in my small hometown and bought a cabin in the Great Smoky Mountains. I guess I'm just trying to fill my shoes."

"Wow. Leave all the mountains behind?"

"I still get one mountain. My favorite one."

"If you change your mind, let me know. Or if you want to stick closer to home, I have a lot of contacts in the park. The Law Enforcement Rangers have jurisdictions. And it wouldn't interfere with dating a colleague who may or may not work for the PNK9 unit."

Nick sighed. "I'm not seeing Officer Orton."

"Maybe not yet. But I saw the interest you have in her. She's pretty and she's smart. That's like chocolate and peanut butter. You can't beat the combination."

Ruby was pretty incredible. Speaking of…she should have been back by now. "That sounds pretty tempting."

"Ruby, a Reese's cup or the job?" Zeke joked.

All of the above, if he was being honest. "The job."

"Let me put a bug in a few ears. Wouldn't hurt to at least fill out an application."

True. What would that hurt? Except his swelling hope. Could he handle abduction cases that happened in the park? Would it be too much? Would the nightmares return? "I'll pray about it."

"Best course of action, bruh. If I hear any more on the case or that partial print, I'll let you know."

"Thanks." He ended the call. Now. Where was Ruby? After switching off the lamp, he absently tousled the doll's head that poked out from underneath the covers and jerked his hand away from the fake hair. Habit. He ached to have his daughter back.

"Goldie, stay." He needed the dog's silhouette in the shadow of the night-light. Everything needed to follow the routine. Needed to be just right.

What wasn't right was that Ruby wasn't here. He called but got no answer. They'd been together like glue for over a week. When this case was gone he wouldn't be spending every day with her, seeing her each day, and that did a number on his heart.

He left Zoe's room, leaving it ajar, and slipped through the dark house. With the boarded windows, it was especially dark. Eerie. Didn't feel like the cozy home he knew it to be.

He grabbed his weapon and Maglite, then exited the kitchen door on the side of the house near the driveway. The night was still. The moon only a thumbprint. He felt watched. Candy? Someone else? Who else was left? Their two main suspects were dead. Candy's prints were on the shovel. Two weeks ago, he'd have ignored that. Candy was in that shed often. Used the shovel often. But now, with her strange behavior and disappearance, he wasn't sure those prints were innocently placed. Her phone call came back to his mind. She'd needed more time. Time to what? Whom had she been talking to? They hadn't had enough concrete evidence to prove Candy was involved in the kidnapping, therefore without probable cause they hadn't been able to get a warrant for her phone records. Sketchy behavior wasn't probable cause.

But now with the prints on the shovel that killed Aaron Millsap and the fact that she'd received large sums of money that had been withdrawn before she disappeared, that would be enough. If tonight didn't pan out the way they suspected it would, then first thing in the morning, they'd be able to secure a warrant for her phone records.

Sticking close to the side of the house, Nick surveyed the property and took extra care to study the ground outside Zoe's bedroom window. Didn't appear that anyone had been lurking. Still, Nick couldn't shake the feeling of being watched.

He rounded the corner when something hard slammed against his head.

And then he saw nothing.

FIFTEEN

Ruby gripped the steering wheel of the truck that the manager at the Stehekin Lodge loaned her. She had to get to Nick. Now more than ever she was thankful that Zoe wasn't here and was at a safe house. But that meant Nick wasn't in the clear, and maybe Goldie, too. Pepper sat beside her in the cab of the truck, her tongue lolling as Ruby rounded the bend and spotted Nick's home and the stables beyond.

Instinct said cut the headlights, so she did and then parked on the side of the road. "Okay, girl, let's move quietly." She exited the truck and Pepper silently jumped out behind her. Grabbing her gun, she moved slowly but smoothly up the road and toward the house.

The crisp air chilled her throat as she inhaled and adrenaline raced through her veins as she hurried up the drive. She paused, listening.

Nothing out of the ordinary.

She knocked on the front door. No answer. She turned the knob. Locked. Why wasn't Nick answering the door? She rounded the house and found the kitchen door ajar. She swallowed hard and began clearing the house as she moved toward Zoe's room.

Inside the room, a woman stood over the bed, Goldie beside her.

"Put your hands up. Slowly."

The woman obeyed. "It's me. Candy Reynolds. I don't have a weapon. I'm not hurting anyone. Where is Zoe? This isn't Zoe."

Candy. She'd suspected the woman would show. Ruby had only hoped she and Nick would have been in here to catch her before she discovered the doll. "You think we'd let you harm her?"

"I would never harm Zoe. I love her. Where is she? Where is Nick?" Confusion flooded her voice.

Good question. Ruby wasn't buying her innocent act. She'd been caught. "How did you get in?" Ruby glanced behind Candy, seeing the window open.

"The kitchen door was unlocked. I'm turning around." Deliberately, Candy turned to face Ruby. "I can explain everything."

"So can I. You were obsessed with Zoe. So much so you somehow got into cahoots with Aaron Millsap and planned this whole thing. Aaron gets revenge on Nick and you get Zoe. You need help, Candy. I can get you help." This wasn't a cold-blooded, cutthroat killer. It was a woman unhinged and in need of medical care. But she would have to pay for her crimes, including two murders and several attempted murder charges.

"No, that's not true. I did hurt Nick. Not in the way you're thinking."

"Where is he?" The fact that he wasn't in the house and the window was open sent a wave of panic through her veins. "What have you done to him? How did you hurt him?"

Candy's eyes widened and her lips trembled. "I've

been taking payments from Luca Hattaway. His rival from Lake Chelan Stables. I've been telling customers we're booked so they'll go to him and he paid me to sabotage the outfitter."

The holes in the fence. The horses getting out. The little things Nick said were adding up to big costs. "Was it you who attacked me that night the horses got out?"

She shook her head. "No. I never hurt you or Nick or Zoe. I just wanted the money to help me and Garrett have a baby. Luca wanted a list of Nick's clients but with everything going on I needed more time. Nick was being extra cautious. I thought he suspected—I didn't realize he thought I'd be guilty of taking Zoe, of hurting him physically."

Ruby kept her gun trained on Candy, but she needed to find Nick. She wasn't sure she believed Candy's story but parts of it did make sense. Luca Hattaway had been steaming mad at Nick and all his success. She wouldn't put it past the guy.

"When I realized the mess I'd made and that someone was trying to kidnap Zoe and kill Nick, I suspected Luca and I got scared. I packed up our camping gear and hid for a while to figure out what to do. I was afraid Luca might kill me, and the less Garrett knew, the safer he'd be, so I didn't tell him. And I couldn't tell Nick my suspicions because then he'd know how much I betrayed him and he's like family to me." Tears leaked from her eyes, spilling down her cheeks, and her raised hands sagged a little.

"Why are you here? In Zoe's room?" Her gut said Candy was telling the truth, but she'd been a shoddy judge of character lately.

"I told you. I was looking for Nick to tell him the truth. I withdrew all the money Luca had given me and gave it back tonight. I wanted no part. I was going to tell Nick, then tell Garrett the truth. I may lose everything but I have to tell the truth."

Ruby wasn't going to drop her guard or her gun. Candy's sob story felt legit and they knew that the money had been withdrawn, as she'd said. But it wasn't her job to guess. The evidence told the story. "Do you know, or were ever approached by, Jeremy Benedict or Aaron Millsap?"

She nodded slowly. "Jeremy. He hated working for Luca. All his promises to Jeremy about having a say were empty. He wanted to come back. He saw me and Luca outside the stables and at Luca's business, and asked if I was leaving Cascades Stables and that he wanted me to put in a good word for him before he came to beg for his job back, but he died before I got the chance." Tears leaked from her eyes.

So Jeremy Benedict was coming to ask Nick for his job back, as they'd suspected. "If you didn't kill him, who did?"

The sounds of shoes scuffling on hardwood sounded and then gunfire exploded, ringing in Ruby's ears.

Candy dropped to the floor, blood seeping through her shirt. Ruby gasped and started to turn, but something hard whacked her—a baseball bat—and knocked the gun from her hands.

"Don't even think about moving."

Ruby stared into the face of the older woman she'd seen talking to Lola Montana at Rainbow Falls. The woman who had looked like an older version of Candy. She recognized her from a photo—though years had formed creases around her blue eyes and a few streaks of gray through her blond hair at the roots.

But there was no mistake that she was peering into

the eyes of Hailey Alan, Nick and Lizzie's old babysitter. She'd gone off the grid after her divorce. And she, too, had fertility issues. Ruby had been right about the motive behind taking Zoe—an unhinged woman who desperately wanted a child. She'd just gotten the woman wrong.

"Don't move," Hailey said. "Where is Zoe?"

Hailey had come tonight to kidnap her, opening the window then getting stalled by Candy, who had shown up at the kitchen door.

"Where is Nick?" She tossed a glance to Candy, who was lying deathly still, blood leaking from her body.

"You don't need to worry about Nick. He got what he deserved. He didn't protect Lizzie and he can't protect Zoe. I saw a newspaper article about his horse outfitter— he was standing there with Zoe and I was shocked. He didn't deserve a child after what he let happen to Lizzie. I kept her safe when I babysat. Just like I kept Molly safe. But my parents asked my brother to watch her and I was in my room. I trusted him. But he got busy and Molly got outside and into the pool. He didn't protect her, either."

She'd lost two young girls she loved. "I'm sorry for that. And I'm sorry you struggled to have a child. But Nick was only eight. He was a child himself. Your sister's drowning was an accident."

Hailey shook her head and her hand trembled. "I thought that might be true. So I tested Nick. He failed."

That's why Zoe wasn't taken. She'd paid Lola Montana to distract Nick, then she took Zoe to see if she could. To see if Nick had changed and would protect Zoe. In Hailey's fragile mind, he'd failed, so she decided to exact punishment by killing him and taking Zoe because she believed she could protect her and keep her safe.

"Let me help Candy. She didn't do anything. I need to see if she's alive."

"No! I said don't move. Where is she?" Hailey demanded. "Where is Zoe?"

"She's safe." She played into her fractured perception. "Away from Nick."

"With that woman agent who's been staying here. I've been watching the house. Keeping close. I saw that man. He was going to ruin my plans."

Aaron Millsap.

"I heard him on the phone to someone, talking about getting even with Nick. I guess he put him away or something but I couldn't have him mess things up for me."

"So you hit him with a shovel from the shed where you'd been hiding out." Those were her footprints. Hailey was almost as tall as Ruby, and that meant her shoe size was large for a woman of average height. They'd assumed it had been a man.

"I stole a key from her key ring." She pointed to Candy, who wasn't speaking or moving. *God, let her be alive! Help her hold on.*

So Aaron Millsap was here and planning revenge, but he didn't know that Hailey had volatile plans, too. She'd ended Aaron before he could end Nick, bringing in even more agents and removing Zoe.

"And Jeremy Benedict?"

Hailey's eyes squinted. "The man in the woods? He saw me with the gun and asked me a lot of questions. I had no choice."

So Hailey Alan had killed both men, and made the attempts on Nick and Ruby's lives, as well as tried to kidnap Zoe.

Ruby was terrified to ask the next question. "Did you kill Nick?"

Hailey exhaled. "Yes. Now tell me where she is or I'll kill you, too."

Ruby's lips trembled. It wouldn't matter if she told her or not. Either way, she was a dead woman. Zoe was without a father and it was her fault. Nick was dead. He died trying to protect his daughter and she hoped Zoe would know that. Be told that and be safe. She'd never be able to thank him for his courage or sacrificial love.

And Ruby would never be able to profess the truth— that she loved him. In the short time they'd been with one another, day in and day out, she'd seen what a godly man, a man who loved wholeheartedly and devotedly without selfishness, looked like.

He looked an awful lot like Jesus in the way he loved.

If only she'd met him earlier. Been clearer about her feelings.

Now, it was over. Lost.

"Tell me where she is!"

Hailey fired the gun and the bullet ripped into Ruby's flesh, sending a blazing fire through her body. She grabbed her shoulder.

"Next time, I hit the heart."

Her heart had already been shattered when she found out Nick was dead.

"Where did they take Zoe?"

This was it.

"I don't know."

She braced herself for the bullet.

Nick hobbled to the kitchen door, his hair matted in blood, a huge goose egg sprouting bigger each second and blinding pain blurring his vision. He'd been cracked hard and likely left for dead, but thank God he hadn't died.

He pushed open the kitchen door as the sound of gunfire exploded in the back of the house.

Zoe's room.

Ruby! Ruby must be back. Oh, no. He pushed through the agonizing pain as the past week fired scenarios into his brain. All of Ruby and her kindness, compassion and wit. He even loved her compulsive need to run a lint brush over hers or anyone's pant legs that had dog hair. It was endearing.

But she might be dead.

He grabbed a knife from the butcher block. Not the best weapon to take to gunfight, but he had no choice. Whoever had knocked him senseless had taken his or tossed it. Either way, he was weaponless. He had no time to get to his bedroom and the shooter would see him in the hallway, anyway. He'd never make it in time.

He prayed for grace and protection, and kept his back to the hallway.

Inside, he heard a woman's voice. Familiar but not Ruby's or Candy's. He worked to place it but his brain was fuzzy from the hit.

Then relief flooded his soul as he heard Ruby's voice, but it was faint and laced with pain. She must have been shot. He had no choice. He had to go in. Try to save her, save them both.

Then it dawned. He knew exactly where he'd heard that voice.

Because it belonged to his old babysitter, Hailey.

"I want answers," she demanded. "I can take care of Zoe. I'll watch over her. Protect her. She'll be the daughter I never had the chance to have and raise. You don't know the pain I've had to endure."

He put the knife into his back pocket to hide it. "Hailey," Nick said softly and stepped into the doorway, hands up in surrender. "Hailey Alan."

She kept her gun on Ruby and looked at Nick. "I thought you were dead. You will be now."

Hailey's eyes were glazed and she made no rational sense. There would be no reasoning with her. She hadn't thought this through. They'd track whatever gun she was using and find her. At some point. This was not going to end well for any of them.

But he had to think of a way to keep her talking. How did one reason with the unreasonable?

"You're right," he said, taking a slow step forward. He only needed to be within striking distance to disarm her. But he had to get there and that was about five feet away.

"About what?" She cocked her head.

"Me. Sean—your brother. We should have done a better job. Every day I've lived with the heaviness of what I did. I regret it. I can't change it. I'm sorry it happened and I'm sorry I hurt you." He wasn't lying and he hoped she wouldn't see this as some kind of ploy.

"I loved her, Nicky." She used her pet name for him. She was the only one who ever called him that.

"I did, too, Hailey. You know I did. You saw us play together. Saw me play tea party when I didn't want to be sipping out of doll cups, but I loved her. I ruined my family."

He took two more slow steps toward her.

"Why didn't you apologize then?" she asked. Tears brimmed from her eyes.

"I didn't know how. I was only eight. But I've been sorry every single day. Just like I know Sean was."

"I deserve a child of my own!"

He glanced at Candy, lying in a crumpled heap on the floor. She'd wanted children, too. He had no clue why she was here, how she fit into this, but she didn't deserve this. "You're right. You do. I don't know why you can't. And I'm sorry for that as well. I truly am."

"It's not fair. I'd be a good mom and wouldn't lose them or let them drown. My brother has four kids and he let my sister die. You—you have beautiful Zoe and you don't deserve her. It's not fair. I read about women hurting and murdering their children and they just keep popping them out like its nothing. Taking it for granted and not wanting them. And it's all I ever wanted!" Tears rolled down her cheeks and she began to lower her weapon.

"I wish I knew why these things happened. I don't. I wish it wasn't this way. Truly."

One more step forward. She righted her gun. "Not another step forward. Not one." She sniffed. "Tell me where Zoe is." She pointed the gun back at Ruby, who had been quiet. She had a wound to her left shoulder and one on her calf. There was too much blood. He had to move fast.

"I'll tell you. But you have to let me get Ruby and Candy medical help."

She hissed. "You don't know where she is. You're stalling. I'll just wait and bide my time…in Florida. They'll give your parents custody. But they're as guilty as you in my book. I'll see to Zoe's needs. I'll be a good mom."

She swung the gun in his direction.

"Hailey, don't do this."

"Lower your weapon," a voice ordered.

Brandie Weller.

"I'll shoot him."

"No. There's no need to shoot him." Brandie slowly entered the room. "Look at me. Real close."

Nick narrowed his eyes as Brandie inched into the room, her eyes wary but calm. Steady. Hair hung from a loose ponytail, framing her face. "You know me."

Know her?

"Princesses only wake up pretty if they get beauty sleep," Brandie said.

Nick's heart skipped a beat and his stomach bottomed out. Immediate tears filled his eyes.

"Lizzie," Hailey whispered. "Is that…is that you?"

Reality hit Nick with full force. *That's* where he'd heard that phrase before. He'd have remembered if Mom had said it every night, but it wasn't Mom. It was Hailey. She'd told Lizzie that to get her to take her naps.

"It's me." She cut Nick a side-eye. "I'm Lizzie Rossi. Though I just recently figured it out."

"How? I thought you were dead," Hailey said.

Nick was too stunned to speak. He had so many questions. Did Ruby know? How did Brandie know? Was that why she was here?

"The couple that kidnapped me from Lake Chelan died and I found some things in the attic that made me wonder if I'd been taken. So I started digging into cold cases. While working Zoe's case, I had a vivid memory near Lake Chelan. And then…" She glanced at Nick and back to Hailey. "I took a cup Nick threw in the trash and sent it off to a private lab. I just read the results in my email. It's a familial match. I am Lizzie Rossi. So you don't need to kill Nick."

"He didn't protect you."

"I *didn't* protect you," he whispered, stunned at the news. Shock kept his body as still as a statue.

"You were eight and it wasn't your job," Brandie said with compassion in her eyes. "And I know most children taken end in tragedy, but my abductors never harmed me."

Nick hiccupped a cry but refrained from saying a word. He had no words.

"It's over, Hailey. Drop the gun. Let's make everything right. We have that chance." Brandie stepped into her personal space, where Nick hadn't been able to. With a quick move of her hands, she disarmed Hailey and handed Nick the gun, then Hailey embraced her and sobbed on her shoulders.

"It's really you."

"It's really me."

Nick raced to Ruby. "Are you okay? We're getting you help right now, Ruby... I love you. Stay with me."

Ruby looked up, her eyes cloudy. "I love you, too."

Then she went limp in his arms.

SIXTEEN

Ruby's arm had been in a sling for the past two weeks. The wound to her calf had only been a flesh wound that needed a few stitches. After Hailey Alan had surrendered, everything was a whirlwind.

Nick had called the ambulance. Hailey had been taken into custody. She'd have to await trial for attempted murder, murder and attempted kidnapping, but with her mental instability the court would likely show mercy and get her what she needed most. Mental-health support.

Once she'd been taken, Nick had wrapped his arms around Lizzie and they'd cried a long time, which had moved Ruby to her own tears. Seeing a family reunited was sadly the exception when it came to child abductions. Then Ruby and Candy had been taken by plane to the nearest hospital. Candy had needed surgery but she survived.

She was now home and her husband had forgiven her, but they were seeking some marital counseling. Only yesterday, Candy had finally visited Nick to come clean about her taking money from Luca Hattaway. While Luca had nothing to do with the murders, he was a real slime ball and when other businesses had found out, he closed up shop. Now there were only three outfitters in Stehekin.

Friends and family had come by Nick's house to welcome Lizzie to the community, though she was still going by Brandie, and as far as Ruby knew planned to. After all, she hadn't been Lizzie Rossi since she was three years old. Jasmin, their tech analyst, did a deeper dig after Nick's DNA evidence returned, and the birth certificate Brandie's parents had used was a fake and had made her a whole year younger, which is why that kept throwing them off. Jasmin said the guy she knew who specialized in forgeries said it was a really good one. They'd used a deceased child's social security number. They'd never know who her parents used, or why they'd taken her. But she was now home with family and where she belonged.

Ruby had gone back to headquarters to give a briefing in person and the chief had given her time off to heal. Mama had flown in and babied her, which she'd loved. They'd had long talks and even longer naps. She had only spoken to Nick a handful of times, but their conversations were short and they hadn't brought up the three words they'd spoken to one another before she was hospitalized. But by phone wasn't the way to do it, anyway. For now, she wanted him to have lots of time to catch up with Brandie. But, oh, she missed him and Zoe fiercely.

For now, she had memories of them and memories of him at the hospital replayed a lot in her head. He'd held her hand while she'd dozed. Each time she awoke while in the hospital, he'd been there. After she was released, he saw her off at the floatplane, giving her one chaste kiss but a deeply meaningful gaze. It was all they had time for with so many PNK9 onlookers and Zoe being there. They just hadn't found the time to really talk about them or a future or what they'd said to each other. But when she was better, she was going to see him. Have a deep conversation.

And tell him she loved him again.

Then she was going to get her hands on the little girl she'd also fallen in love with. Zoe had been reunited with her dad and now Aunt Brandie. They hadn't told her about the abduction, only that it was a fun surprise that Brandie was his sister. Children would believe anything without question, which made child abduction so easy. So frightening.

Not all of Brandie's memories had come back, but once her identity had been confirmed by DNA, she had a memory of a girl telling her it was naptime and the phrase about the princess. Brandie had taken a chance when she'd repeated it that night, hoping Hailey was indeed the babysitter. She hadn't really been sure.

It had paid off.

Ruby's mama was now gone. Ruby wasn't fully recovered, but she was able to hobble around on her own. She checked the time on her cell phone. She had a video conference with the team in two minutes.

After logging in, she chatted with the team, filling them in on her recovery and thanking them for their gifts and coming over the past two weeks to see her. They were the family she had chosen.

Finally, the chief took over. "Asher is going to brief everyone on where we stand in Mara's case."

Asher Gilmore cleared his throat. "After our interview with Eli Ballard, you know that Layla's dog, Bixby, alerted at the Stark Lodge. We knew there were guns. Tanner and I later went back, taking a chance and hoping the manager might give us permission to go down there and see for ourselves if it was family guns as Eli said. He let us."

"And?" Ruby asked.

Some of the team made faces that told Ruby they already knew what happened. Ruby was in the dark.

"We were played," Asher said. "Ruby, with your injuries and being in the hospital, we thought it would be a good idea to wait to tell you."

Eli. She'd been wrong about him. A total idiot. "Eli's behind this, isn't he?"

"We don't know for sure. The night manager however is. Brad Sheffield let us go down into the basement. There were several crates of guns and a few rifles on the wall. It's possible Eli was telling us the truth and had no idea that Brad was using the lodge to store guns. But while we were down there, Brad opened fire. Maybe at Eli's command. Maybe not. But guess who was Eli's alibi for the date and time of Stacey Stark's and Jonas Digby's murders?"

Ruby gasped. Brad Sheffield.

"Was anyone hurt?" Ruby asked. She couldn't even be mad they'd kept this from her until now. She'd had a lot to deal with.

"No. And Sheffield got away. We went to Eli's to talk to him. See if he was in on it with Brad or unaware. At this point, we still really don't know. It looks *really* bad for Eli, but it's circumstantial. He wasn't home, so we went back to the lodge, knowing Brad wouldn't be dumb enough to return. The guns had been cleared out. At Brad's request? Eli's? We aren't sure. And we won't be until we have the chance to talk to Eli and to find Brad. He's on the run. But we'll find him."

So Eli *might* be innocent. She hoped so, but it was doubtful. It didn't matter anymore. She wasn't going to worry about what she might look like for having dated him. She had made some bad calls in relationships. But no more.

"And the puppies?"

"We leave tomorrow," Chief said. "Had some prep work that took more time. But Asher and I are heading to Salt Creek Recreation Area near Port Angeles and Olympic National Park."

Gun runners. Drug runners. Puppy thieves. They really had their work cut out. "Be careful. Keep us updated."

"We will. You'll all be on standby in case we do end up needing backup."

After she ended the call, the doorbell rang.

Nick stood on her doorstep and her heart took flight. He wasn't supposed to be here; he was supposed to be spending time with his sister and family.

She grinned and let him inside. "What on earth are you doing here?" she asked. She had one more week of recovery then she was going to ring his doorbell.

"I missed you." His grin sent her heart into a puddle. "How are you feeling?"

"Much better."

"Good." He held her gaze, his eyes searching hers. He swallowed hard and touched her cheek. "I know we said we'd wait to talk, but I can't wait. I love you. I meant what I said and while I adore your sacrificing nature, to give up time so that I could focus on Brandie... I just couldn't wait. Maybe I'm selfish." He grinned and she felt like she was spinning off into a glorious horizon.

"I love you, too, and waiting has been killing me, but... I do want you to have time with Brandie. Y'all have been apart far too long."

"And I'm going to have her in my life again. I want you

back in it, too. Right now." He embraced her and gently kissed her.

"So I was wondering if you might want to finish out your last week of recovery in Stehekin. We can fly or ferry. Your call."

She cocked her head. Before she was working a case. Just spending a week with him now that they'd declared their love seemed awkward.

He laughed. "I see that look. My parents are flying in later today and I want you there to meet them, get to know them."

"You want me to meet your parents?"

"Ruby," Nick said and kissed one cheek and then the other one, "I'm going to marry you. I know it like I know the back of my hand. And clearly, when I know what I want, I don't do patient well. So, yeah. Will you? Brandie's going to stay, too. She took a leave of absence from work. She'll still be trying out for the program but she's going to stay with me, too."

She wrapped her arms around his neck and clung to him tightly. "Then I guess there's nothing to do but say yes."

"Daddy, I couldn't wait!" Zoe rushed into Ruby's house and that's when she saw Brandie standing at the car waving.

"Officer Ruby! I'm back from my big trip."

"I want to hear all about it." Ruby let Nick help her to the couch then Zoe snuggled up next to her, Goldie and Pepper nosing each other like old comrades.

"I missed you," Zoe said.

"I missed you, too. So much. I love you, punkin."

Zoe patted her leg with her little hand. "Daddy said you gots hurt."

"I did." She smoothed Zoe's hair. "But I'm almost all better now and I'm going to come and stay with you."

Zoe raised her fists in a victory pump. "Yay!"

She looked over at Nick and couldn't believe that God had been so good to her, to give her this man full of integrity and honor, and the most precious little girl. And another dog!

Her mama had been right. When it was God's time, He'd make a way.

And He surely made a way for Ruby.

* * * * *

Don't miss Asher Gilmore's story,
Undercover Operation, *and the rest of*
the Pacific Northwest K-9 Unit series:

Shielding the Baby
by Laura Scott, April 2023

Scent of Truth
by Valerie Hansen, May 2023

Explosive Trail
by Terri Reed, June 2023

Olympic Mountain Pursuit
by Jodie Bailey, July 2023

Threat Detection
by Sharon Dunn, August 2023

Cold Case Revenge
by Jessica R. Patch, September 2023

Undercover Operation
by Maggie K. Black, October 2023

Snowbound Escape
by Dana Mentink, November 2023

K-9 National Park Defenders
by Katy Lee and Sharee Stover, December 2023

Dear Reader,

Thank you for reading Nick and Ruby's story. I hope you enjoyed the real setting of Stehekin and will give me grace if you're from there or have visited for stretching and changing a few places for the story's sake. Ruby and Nick have to deal with their pasts, which are complicated like most of our pasts. We carry guilt we shouldn't and make choices that aren't good for us, but God is a good Father and He loves us, forgives us, and Christ carried our guilt and shame on the cross so we don't have to bear that burden now. I love to stay connected to you! Sign up for my monthly newsletter and get "Patched In" at www.jessicarpatch.com and join in the fun conversations on my Facebook page at Jessica R. Patch. Until next time, may the unfailing love of God surround you like a shield!

Warmly,
Jessica

COMING NEXT MONTH FROM
Love Inspired Suspense

UNDERCOVER OPERATION
Pacific Northwest K-9 Unit • by Maggie K. Black
After three bloodhound puppies are stolen, K-9 officer Asher Gilmore and trainer Peyton Burns are forced to go undercover as married drug smugglers to rescue them. But infiltrating the criminals will be more dangerous than expected, putting the operation, the puppies and their own lives at risk.

TRACKED THROUGH THE WOODS
by Laura Scott
Abby Miller is determined to find her missing FBI informant father before the mafia does, but time is running out. Can she trust special agent Wyatt Kane to protect her from the gunmen on her trail, to locate her father—and to uncover an FBI mole?

HUNTED AT CHRISTMAS
Amish Country Justice • by Dana R. Lynn
When single mother Addison Johnson is attacked by a hit man, she learns there's a price on her head. Soon it becomes clear that Isaiah Bender—the bounty hunter hired to track her down for crimes she didn't commit—is her only hope for survival.

SEEKING JUSTICE
by Sharee Stover
With her undercover operation in jeopardy, FBI agent Tiandra Daugherty replaces her injured partner with his identical twin brother, Officer Elijah Kenyon. But saving her mission puts Elijah in danger. Can Tiandra and her K-9 keep him alive before he becomes the next target?

RESCUING THE STOLEN CHILD
by Connie Queen
When Texas Ranger Zane Adcock's grandson is kidnapped and used as leverage to get Zane to investigate an old murder case, he calls his ex-fiancée for help. Zane and retired US marshal Bliss Walker will risk their lives to take down the criminals...and find the missing boy before it's too late.

CHRISTMAS MURDER COVER-UP
by Shannon Redmon
After Detective Liz Burke finds her confidential informant dead and interrupts the killer's escape, she's knocked unconscious and struggles to remember the details of the murder. With a target on her back, she must team up with homicide detective Oz Kelly to unravel a deadly scheme—and stay alive.

———

LOOK FOR THESE AND OTHER LOVE INSPIRED BOOKS WHEREVER BOOKS ARE SOLD, INCLUDING MOST BOOKSTORES, SUPERMARKETS, DISCOUNT STORES AND DRUGSTORES.

LISCNM0823

Get 3 FREE REWARDS!

We'll send you 2 FREE Books plus a FREE Mystery Gift.

FREE
Value Over
$20

Both the **Love Inspired®** and **Love Inspired® Suspense** series feature compelling novels filled with inspirational romance, faith, forgiveness and hope.

YES! Please send me 2 FREE novels from the Love Inspired or Love Inspired Suspense series and my FREE gift (gift is worth about $10 retail). After receiving them, if I don't wish to receive any more books, I can return the shipping statement marked "cancel." If I don't cancel, I will receive 6 brand-new Love Inspired Larger-Print books or Love Inspired Suspense Larger-Print books every month and be billed just $6.49 each in the U.S. or $6.74 each in Canada. That is a savings of at least 16% off the cover price. It's quite a bargain! Shipping and handling is just 50¢ per book in the U.S. and $1.25 per book in Canada.* I understand that accepting the 2 free books and gift places me under no obligation to buy anything. I can always return a shipment and cancel at any time by calling the number below. The free books and gift are mine to keep no matter what I decide.

Choose one:
☐ **Love Inspired Larger-Print** (122/322 BPA GRPA)
☐ **Love Inspired Suspense Larger-Print** (107/307 BPA GRPA)
☐ **Or Try Both!** (122/322 & 107/307 BPA GRRP)

Name (please print)

Address _____ Apt. #

City _____ State/Province _____ Zip/Postal Code

Email: Please check this box ☐ if you would like to receive newsletters and promotional emails from Harlequin Enterprises ULC and its affiliates. You can unsubscribe anytime.

Mail to the **Harlequin Reader Service:**
IN U.S.A.: P.O. Box 1341, Buffalo, NY 14240-8531
IN CANADA: P.O. Box 603, Fort Erie, Ontario L2A 5X3

Want to try 2 free books from another series? Call 1-800-873-8635 or visit www.ReaderService.com

*Terms and prices subject to change without notice. Prices do not include sales taxes, which will be charged (if applicable) based on your state or country of residence. Canadian residents will be charged applicable taxes. Offer not valid in Quebec. This offer is limited to one order per household. Books received may not be as shown. Not valid for current subscribers to the Love Inspired or Love Inspired Suspense series. All orders subject to approval. Credit or debit balances in a customer's account(s) may be offset by any other outstanding balance owed by or to the customer. Please allow 4 to 6 weeks for delivery. Offer available while quantities last.

Your Privacy—Your information is being collected by Harlequin Enterprises ULC, operating as Harlequin Reader Service. For a complete summary of the information we collect, how we use this information and to whom it is disclosed, please visit our privacy notice located at corporate.harlequin.com/privacy-notice. From time to time we may also exchange your personal information with reputable third parties. If you wish to opt out of this sharing of your personal information, please visit readerservice.com/consumerschoice or call 1-800-873-8635. **Notice to California Residents**—Under California law, you have specific rights to control and access your data. For more information on these rights and how to exercise them, visit corporate.harlequin.com/california-privacy.

LIRLIS23

HARLEQUIN
PLUS

Try the best multimedia
subscription service for romance
readers like you!

Read, Watch and Play.

Experience the easiest way to get
the romance content you crave.

Start your **FREE TRIAL** at
<u>www.harlequinplus.com/freetrial</u>.